THE
POPULARITY PACT
SCHOOL
SQUAD

❧ BOOK TWO ❧

EILEEN MOSKOWITZ-PALMA

RP | KIDS
PHILADELPHIA

FOR MY FATHER, THE TOUGH FIRE CAPTAIN WHO WASN'T AFRAID TO TAKE ME PROM DRESS SHOPPING

Running Press Kids
Hachette Book Group
1290 Avenue of the Americas, New York, NY 10104
www.runningpress.com/rpkids
@RP_Kids

Printed in the United States of America

First Trade Paperback Edition: August 2021

Published by Running Press Kids, an imprint of Perseus Books, LLC, a subsidiary of Hachette Book Group, Inc. The Running Press Kids name and logo is a trademark of the Hachette Book Group.

The Hachette Speakers Bureau provides a wide range of authors for speaking events. To find out more, go to www.hachettespeakersbureau.com or call (866) 376-6591.

The publisher is not responsible for websites (or their content) that are not owned by the publisher.

Print book cover and interior design by Marissa Raybuck.

Library of Congress Control Number: 2019946931

ISBNs: 978-0-7624-6748-8 (paperback), 978-0-7624-6750-1 (hardcover), 978-0-7624-6747-1 (ebook)

LSC-C

Printing 1, 2021

⇥∙∙ CHAPTER ONE ∙∙⇤

BEA

"I NEVER WANT TO GET OFF THIS BUS." I WATCHED THE LAST
Burger King before the Mapleton exit pass by in a swirl of red and
orange, the rich scent of greasy burgers and salty fries wafting
through the open window.

Maisy focused her eyes on me. "It's going to be okay," she said.

I broke her gaze and looked down at my thighs. They were
covered with so many freckle constellations, I almost looked tan.
"Things are about as far from okay as you can get. My dad's replac-
ing my mom and me with new and improved models. My mom's
dating our old math teacher, and I'm about to start middle school
with zero friends."

"That last part's not true," Maisy said, as she held out a practically empty bag of Sour Patch Kids. "You have me."

I popped a yellow candy in my mouth and felt the sour sugar crystals burn my tongue before the candy turned sweet.

"I can't expect you to give up the popular table for me," I said midchew. "So, if you want me, I'll be eating tuna sandwiches alone in the library."

"Tuna?" Maisy scrunched up her face. "No wonder no one wanted to sit with you."

"It's not funny. School starts in two days and I'm going to be just as invisible as I was last year," I moaned.

"You held up your end of the pact and made me, the least athletic and most anxious girl at adventure camp, popular. Now it's *my* turn to make *you* popular at school."

"How did I ever think we could pull this off?" I asked. "How could I ever fit in with the M & Ms?" The bus pulled off the highway onto the red maple tree–lined street that ran through the center of Mapleton. The other campers laughed and talked as if the end of the summer wasn't descending upon us like an apocalyptic plague. They may have been sad to say goodbye to the summer, but clearly they all had friends back home they were eager to see.

"We just need to come up with another plan," Maisy said. "So, put that freakishly big brain of yours to work."

I grabbed the last Sour Patch Kid. "I've got nothing."

Maisy licked her finger and ran it along the inside of the bag. "Let's list all the things we know about the situation. My dad says to do that when I'm stuck on a word problem, which is pretty much every time I do math homework."

"There's unpopular, and then there's the level below unpopular, where you're so invisible, you aren't on anyone's radar to merit the label unpopular. That's what we're working with."

Maisy rolled her eyes. "And you call me dramatic?"

"Fine, I'll play along." I cleared my throat. "Here are the known variables. Having the right friend group is the key to middle school survival. If I can get in with the M & Ms, I won't have to spend the school year hiding in the bathroom during free periods."

Maisy nodded. "We also know the M & Ms are always out for themselves."

"Exactly." I sighed. "Why would they help *me*?"

"We just need to figure out what's in it for them," said Maisy. "There must be something they could get out of being friends with you."

But I couldn't think of one thing those girls needed, especially Mia, whose popularity was matched by her Queen Bee wardrobe. I thought about Madeline with her gel manis and hair even Beyoncé would envy. Then there were Meghan and Madison, who had the kind of friendship born of having moms who were lifelong best friends. Having a person who is more family than friend is the kind of safety net that can make the difference between middle school survival and failure. Let's not forget Chloe Bradford-Fuller, who had swooped in and snatched up the spot in the group Maisy had carved out for me. These girls had everything I wanted. What could I possibly give them?

Maisy whipped her hair into a french braid at record speed. Anytime Maisy is freaking out, she plays with her hair, so this was a surefire sign she wasn't as confident about our strategizing as she was letting on.

"We need to figure out something they might want. Make them realize they want it. Then, convince them you're the only person who can give it to them," Maisy said, as she wrapped a rubber band around the bottom of her braid.

"That's genius." I stared at Maisy. "But what could I possibly give the girls who have everything?"

MAISY

As the bus thumped over the speed bumps in the parking lot, my heart pounded. I was acting calm for Bea, but the closer we got to our real life back home, the more anxious I felt.

It wasn't just about holding up my end of the pact. I needed to make up for ditching Bea last year and ruining her life. I needed to give her the one thing she wanted—a friend group at school, just like she has at camp.

"Mapleton girls!" Bob, our bus driver, called to the back. "This is your stop! Don't leave any garbage behind!"

I shoved the empty chip bags, candy wrappers, and deflated Capri Sun pouches into my bag. Bea and I stood up and brushed the Dorito crumbs and Sour Patch Kids dust off our shorts and grabbed our drawstring bags.

As I walked past the other kids, I heard another bus pull into the parking lot. I leaned out the window to get a closer look.

Bob growled, "Let's go, girls! I still got two more states to drive through today!"

I hurried down the aisle. The parking lot was filled with parents. I put my hand over my eyes to block out the sun and looked around but didn't see Dad or Bea's mom.

"We're the only two kids getting picked up from Camp Amelia," I said. "Why are all these other parents here?"

"This is where all the camps have drop-offs."

Bea sighed as our bus pulled onto the main road. "Just like that. Our summer is over."

"Not true." I dumped my duffel bag down on the hot blacktop. "We still have two days before school starts to figure out our plan."

"There won't be a plan if I can't think of something I can give the M & Ms," Bea said, just as another yellow bus rumbled across the parking lot and pulled up in front of us.

As soon as the bus door opened sweaty boy smell hit us. It was even worse than the time Addy left a pile of dirty leotards in the back of our minivan during a heat wave.

Bea wrinkled her nose. "You thought I had questionable hygiene at camp when I counted swimming in the lake as my shower? You haven't been around when the Scouts get back from their annual camping trip. We're talking about seventh-grade boys running around the woods for two weeks without running water or soap."

I shuddered. "We are so lucky we don't have brothers."

Bea squished up her whole face. "Agreed."

"That smell, though." I tried not to breathe through my nose. "It's like moldy cheese, feet . . . and . . ."

Bea gagged. "Rotten garbage."

I felt a dry heave coming on. "Ugh. That's it."

Bea grabbed my arm and pulled me a few steps back. "Let's give them a wide berth."

"Why do you always have to use big words?" I dragged my stuff back far enough so we could check out the guys without smelling them.

"It's called reading." Bea smirked. "You should try it sometime."

"You are sooo funny," I said.

Marshall Cooper was the first guy off the bus. With his thick glasses strapped around his greasy hair, his dirt-streaked Mapleton School Chess Club T-shirt over cargo shorts, and bright orange Crocs, he could've been cast in any eighties remake as head of the nerd herd.

"Things could be worse." I jerked my head toward the bus as another grubby geek walked off and said, "You could be one of those guys."

Bea shrugged. "At least they have their place in the world."

I rolled my eyes, even though she was right. "We literally just got off the bus. Give me a chance to come up with a new plan before you have a nervous breakdown."

Suddenly, a bright ray of sunshine broke through the fluffy white clouds and shone down on the bus steps. Clark Rutner stepped into the light like a superhero in a Marvel movie. He had gotten teenager tall over the summer, and his tan arms were thick with actual muscles. His red Mapleton Scouts Troop 523 T-shirt stretched across his wide chest. He had grown out his sun-streaked blond hair from a babyish crewcut into a longish surfer-boy hairstyle.

I knocked Bea's arm with my elbow and hissed, "OMG! Do you know what's happening here?"

"Ow!" Bea rubbed her arm. "What? What's happening?"

"Sometimes I wonder how someone *so* smart could be *so* dumb," I whispered. "We are getting the first look at Mapleton Middle School's Summer Glow Up."

Bea wrinkled her forehead and practically shouted, "What the heck is a Glow Up?"

"Keep your voice down," I whispered. "It's when someone goes from the awkward, ugly stage to super cute overnight."

"Oh, now I get it." Bea nodded slowly. "I'm pretty sure Hans Christian Andersen invented that."

"Who?"

Bea threw her hands up. "'The Ugly Duckling'?"

Before I could answer her, Clark turned toward us and smiled. His teeth were bright white and perfect, like a row of peppermint Orbit gum. I was just lifting my arm to wave back when he said, "Hey, Bea."

"How do *you* know the Glow Up?" I asked, trying not to move my lips.

"We were both in accelerated science and math last year," Bea said. "We're in all the honors classes together this year."

I held out my phone and pretended to be taking a selfie. Instead, I got a pic of Clark walking toward us, his blond hair flowing, his golden skin soaking up the sun.

"I think I figured out what you can give the M & Ms," I said.

$\twoheadrightarrow\cdots$ CHAPTER TWO $\cdots\twoheadleftarrow$

BEA

I MAY NOT HAVE KNOWN WHAT GLOW UP MEANT BEFORE, BUT I did now. Last year, Clark had thick glasses, an unfortunate case of acne, and a mouthful of braces. He had reminded me of a puppy, with his giant hands and feet that were too big for the rest of his scrawny body. It was hard to believe the combination of summer sun and puberty resulted in such a dramatic transformation.

Clark had always been nice to me, as much as any sixth-grade boy could be to an invisible girl. Math and science were the only classes where I didn't feel like crawling under my desk when the teacher asked us to partner up because Clark was always happy to work together.

"Did you get the email from Dr. Feinstein about Robotics Club?" Clark asked.

I pointed to my Camp Amelia shirt. "Just got back from a digital detox."

Clark pushed his long blond hair off his forehead. "Dr. Feinstein's starting a robotics club and she reached out to all the honors math and science kids. Check your inbox when you get a chance."

I may not be an expert on how to get popular, but I knew one way to sabotage any chance of improving my social status—joining the Robotics Club.

"I don't think..." I felt a jab in my rib from Maisy's sharp elbow.

"You should definitely join," said Maisy, her furrowed brow a dead giveaway that her brain was currently mid-scheme. "It'll look good on your college application."

Clark raised an eyebrow. "Colleges look at middle school activities now? Mrs. C. said I should join mock trial, but I was going to wait another year so I can focus on my grades."

"Um, well... not exactly," said Maisy. "But how do you expect to be president of Robotics Club in high school if you don't join in middle school?"

"Good point." Clark nodded. "See you at the first meeting, Bea?"

I wasn't exactly sure how this fit into Maisy's plan, but I could practically see the wheels turning in her head.

"Sure," I said.

Mrs. Rutner honked from across the parking lot in her convertible. She was wearing tennis whites and a stressed look on her face.

"Come on, Clark! I'm going to be late for my lesson!"

"See you guys later." Clark took off across the pavement.

As soon as Mrs. Rutner pulled away, Maisy turned to me, her eyes flashing. "Best plan ever, right?"

"I'm going to need a little help connecting the dots," I said.

She whipped out her phone and zoomed in on a picture of Clark 2.0.

"How did you take that without me noticing?" I asked. "And what does our pact have to do with Clark?"

"Watch and learn." Maisy's fingers moved at the speed of light as she sent a group text to the M & Ms with Clark's picture.

From: Maisy
To: Madison, Meghan, Mia, Madeline, Chloe

Back from 🗿 . . . Found Glow Up 🔥 of the Year

Within seconds Maisy's phone beeped.

From: Meghan
To: Maisy, Madison, Mia, Madeline, Chloe

🔥 🔥 🔥 😍 😍

From: Madison
To: Maisy, Meghan, Mia, Madeline, Chloe

🔥 😍 😲

From: Madeline
To: Maisy, Madison, Meghan, Mia, Chloe

OMG! From 🤓 to 👑 🔥

"Wait for it . . ." said Maisy.

From: Mia
To: Maisy, Madeline, Meghan, Madison, Chloe

We need to claim him. Must hang out with 🔥 guys if we want to be 👑 👑 👑 👑 👑

"Bam!" said Maisy.

From: Meghan
To: Maisy, Madeline, Mia, Madison, Chloe

He's literally the smartest kid 🤓 in our school. How do we even talk to him? 🤔

From: Madison
To: Maisy, Madeline, Mia, Meghan, Chloe

He's so 🤓 you practically need Google Translate 📞 to talk to him

"Double bam!" said Maisy. "It couldn't have gone any more perfect than this."

From: Maisy
To: Madison, Meghan, Mia, Madeline, Chloe

We need a Genius Whisperer! 🤓

12

From: Madeline
To: Maisy, Madison, Meghan, Mia, Chloe

A what? 😕

From: Meghan
To: Maisy, Madison, Mia, Madeline, Chloe

Who? 🗿

From: Maisy
To: Madison, Meghan, Mia, Madeline, Chloe

I know the perfect person—someone who will be in all his 🤓 classes so she speaks his language.

From: Madeline
To: Maisy, Madison, Meghan, Mia, Chloe

Who???? 🗿

From: Maisy
To: Madeline, Madison, Meghan, Mia, Chloe

It's a surprise!

From: Mia
To: Maisy, Madison, Meghan, Madeline, Chloe

Bring her to my 🏠 later! 😜

MAISY

Bea paced with her hands clasped over a pile of curls on top of her head. "How can I be a Genius Whisperer when I have no idea how to talk to boys?"

I pointed at myself. "I know how to talk to boys." I pointed at Bea. "You know how to talk to smart people. We'll figure it out."

Bea stopped pacing and slowly turned to face me. "This could actually work."

Bea's mom, Heather, pulled up next to us in her lime-green VW Bug and threw the driver's-side door open.

"Bea!" Heather yelled. She picked Bea up and squeezed her tight.

Heather was wearing turquoise harem pants with a soft gray tank that opened in the back, and when she reached her arms around Bea, you could see the tattoo of a mother and baby elephant across her lower back. She has the same wild curly red hair and pale freckly skin as Bea.

I took a step back because I was sure Heather hated me. I had been awful to Bea last year, and if I were Bea's mother I would definitely hate me. But as soon as Heather was done saying how long Bea's hair had grown and counting her new freckles, she turned to me with a big *I don't hate you* smile.

"Hi, Maisy," she said. "You look great! Wish I had your complexion. I've been slathering myself in SPF one hundred all summer and still got sunburned at the farmers market last weekend. I was there forty-five minutes tops and looked like a lobster by the time I got home."

Bea's mom had been like a second mom to me since preschool.

She taught me how to french braid using Bea's American Girl dolls. She made me chamomile tea with extra clover honey whenever I felt anxious and always knew exactly what to say to make me feel better. She cooked me well-done cheeseburgers even though she and Bea like theirs rare, because she knows I get nervous when there is any pink in my meat. I was really lucky she was talking to me as though I hadn't ruined her daughter's life last year.

"Maisy ran around the cabin spraying everyone with sunblock and bug spray before we went anywhere," said Bea.

I cringed. "Yeah, I think I drove everyone crazy."

"But no one got any bad burns or bug bites the whole summer," Bea said.

"True," I agreed.

Dad pulled up next to us in his Jeep with Grandma in the passenger seat. The Jeep top was down and I could tell by his tan that it had probably been down all summer without me and Addy complaining about Jeep hair.

"Grandma!" I yelled. "What're you doing here? Shouldn't you be getting your classroom ready?"

"Is that any way to greet your grandma?" she teased.

Dad helped her climb out of the Jeep. She's a shorty, like me, so it was a long way down for her. Grandma, who always dresses her best, was wearing fitted white jeans with a turquoise and white tunic and a bright coral necklace. Her gold strappy sandals showed off her perfect pedicure, Essie's Jelly Apple, the color she wears from Memorial Day until the first day of school, when she switches to her fall color, Essie's Merino Cool.

Dad gave me a big bear hug. I thought about how mad I was when he had dropped me off at the camp bus and how I hadn't even hugged him goodbye. I squeezed him extra tight.

"Missed you, Mini," he said. "I didn't have anyone to keep me from being a fashion disaster. My residents made fun of me last week for being too matchy-matchy, whatever that means."

I gave Dad an extra squeeze. "Good thing I'm back."

Dad threw my duffel in the back of the Jeep like it weighed two pounds instead of twenty.

He turned to Bea's mom and said, "Hey, Red. Got any cheap house listings for my poor resident who's drowning in student loans?"

Heather scrunched up her face like she was thinking hard. "Maybe I can set him up with a starter condo with solid resale value so he can turn it around when he gets on his feet."

"Good plan," Dad said. "I'll give him your contact info."

Heather smiled at Dad. "Thanks, Eddy! I owe you big time for connecting me with the head of your department. The commission on that sale is paying for spring break for Bea and me."

Dad waved his hand like it was no big deal. "I wouldn't recommend you if you didn't do a good job."

Heather ran over to Grandma and leaned down to wrap her in a big hug. "Congrats on your retirement, Raisa! I was so excited for you when I saw your Facebook post."

"Thank you! I got the sweetest comments from all the kids I've taught over the years. Although after thirty-nine years of teaching, most of the 'kids' are all grown up now with families of their own."

The tips of my fingers started tingling, like they always do when something doesn't feel right. There's nothing worse than realizing you're the last person to know something important.

"I thought you were retiring next year so we could throw you a big party for teaching forty years," I said.

We had looked at the Party City website last time Grandma visited and decided on black and silver for the party colors and big silver balloons in the shape of a four and a zero. We were even going to special-order a cake that was shaped like a classroom with a little fondant Grandma sitting at her desk.

Grandma pushed her oversized sunglasses on top of her shiny black hair so that I could see her hazel eyes, almond-shaped just like mine, Dad's, and Addy's. She said, "There are more important things than a stupid number. Like spending time with my favorite granddaughters."

I smiled at Grandma, but the pins-and-needles feeling spread to my whole body. The only thing worse than finding something out last is being lied to. Grandma loves visiting us, but she's always loved teaching more.

→··· CHAPTER THREE ···←

BEA

AS SOON AS MOM OPENED THE FRONT DOOR, MR. PEBBLES POUNCED down from the coffee table and rubbed his furry sides against my ankles with a loud purr that sounded like a lawn mower.

"Did you miss me? Did my favorite boy miss me?" I crooned as I scooped him up and flopped down on the couch with him in my arms.

He leaned his head back and parted his lips in a pointy-toothed grin while I rubbed his favorite spot behind his ears.

"Aw, I missed you too," I said.

Mom plopped on the couch, snuggled up next to me, and said, "We're so glad you're back." Her curls tickled my face. They smelled like Moroccan oil and coconut shampoo, a scent that always makes me feel like home.

"Did you hear about Dad and Monica?" I asked.

Mom sat up straighter and pulled her mass of curls out of her face and into an overflowing bun so she could get a better look at me with her big brown eyes. "Your father called me."

"Did you see their proposal video? It's on Instagram," I said.

Mom's mouth twitched. "There's a proposal video?"

I nodded. "Maisy and I saw it when we finally got our phones back."

"And it's on Instagram?" Mom said, before bursting into giggles. "When your dad and I were together he didn't even like me tagging pictures of him on Facebook."

I reached under Mr. Pebbles and grabbed my phone from my jean shorts pocket. "I waited to watch it with you."

Mom put on her reading glasses and leaned closer to my phone. "Why's your dad's proposal video on @morethanmomjeans?"

"Monica's an influencer with half a million followers. Didn't Dad tell you? She posted a denim overall dress from Madewell back in April and it's been backordered for months. She made so much, it paid for Peyton's and Vivi's summer camps."

Mom's eyes widened. "Dad's Monica is the woman behind More Than Mom Jeans? I bought these pants after she posted them. When Jimmy said she was a mom blogger, I thought she was sharing recipes and cutesy posts about her kids."

"How did you miss her engagement post if you're such a big fan?" I asked.

Mom shook her hair loose from her bun so her big curls covered her pink cheeks. "I've been spending so much time with Gavin these days, I haven't been on social media as much."

I was happy Mom had found someone but wished it wasn't my former math teacher who wore bowties and gave detention for chewing gum. Associating with Mr. Pembrook was not going to do my reputation any favors. The only thing saving me was that he taught at the elementary school.

I looked down at my phone and scrolled through Monica's posts till I found the proposal video. "Here it is." I turned up the volume.

Monica stood on the front lawn wearing high-waisted jeans, with a boxy linen button-down and buttery leather loafers. Her blond hair fell in loose waves over her shoulders and her makeup was flawless.

"When I was a kid, I couldn't wait to wear my new back-to-school clothes!" The tiny Monica on the screen smacked her hands together in excitement. "With these budget-friendly finds, the whole family can experience that fresh-start feeling this fall. Peyton and Vivi," her face broke into a wide smile, "and my amazing boyfriend, Jimmy, are going to model for us today."

Mom laughed. "She got your dad to model? This must be true love."

Monica held out her arm. "First, we have Peyton, in Abercrombie and Fitch . . ."

Peyton's only one year older than me, but the puberty gods have been far kinder to her. She has her mom's sun-kissed hair, clear skin, and long legs. Peyton walked across the lawn wearing a fitted white T-shirt with the words WILL YOU painted in bold red across her chest.

Vivi, who is two years younger than Peyton, and as flawless as her mom and sister are, but with a round, friendly face and smile, ran out wearing a white T-shirt with the word MARRY painted on it.

Monica's jaw dropped and she clasped her hands over her cheeks. Before she could say anything, Dad ran over wearing a white shirt that said ME.

"Oh, Jimmy," Monica said, in a breathless voice, as Dad got down on one knee and popped open a ring box.

"You guys!" Tears streamed down Monica's impeccably made-up face as she swept up the girls in a big hug. "I can't believe you did this!"

"You didn't answer the question," Dad said, with his trademark crooked smile.

Monica dropped to her knees so she was at Dad's level. She looked him in the eyes and said, "Yes!" Then her eyes shifted to her four hundred and eighty-nine thousand Instagram followers, and she shouted, "I said yes! The answer is yes!" She then reached out her hand and Dad pushed a platinum and diamond ring on her finger.

Peyton looked at her mom and said, "Now we can be a *real* family."

I put my phone facedown on the coffee table and snuggled up to Mr. Pebbles.

"They make the perfect family, don't they?" I scoffed.

Mom snuggled up closer to me and smoothed my hair down. "There's no such thing as a perfect family. I was at a house closing last week and the family was an absolute nightmare. The three kids were bickering and playing something called the Fart and Sniff Game, which is just as disgusting as it sounds. The parents argued about whether or not to remodel the kitchen and whose mother could come stay first, the *entire* time we were signing the papers. But as soon as everything was signed, the mom made me take pictures of the family sitting on the front steps 'til I got the perfect shot, which she promptly posted on Instagram with #blessed."

Sometimes I want to sit with my negative thoughts without Mom trying to fix things. I handed Mr. Pebbles to Mom and stood up.

"I have to go to the bathroom. Maisy and I drank a whole case of Capri Sun on the bus," I said.

The bathroom was the only room where Mom wouldn't trail behind me. I shut the door, ready to experience the peacefulness of being alone after bunking with four other girls all summer.

But as soon as I set foot in the bathroom, something felt different. I pushed back the elephant print linen shower curtain and noted the caddy was filled with our normal toiletries, but sitting on the rim of the tub was a tube of beard conditioner and two-in-one shampoo and conditioner. There was no way Mom or I could get a brush through our hair if we used two-in-one shampoo and conditioner, and we didn't need beard conditioner, thank goodness.

I tried really hard not to think about Mr. Pembrook naked in my shower. Then, when I thought it couldn't get any worse, I saw a book called *Vegan Gut Health* on the shelf over the toilet. Maisy was definitely going to paper the toilet seat next time she came over.

I needed to clear my head, and an ice-cold glass of chocolate milk is the cure for pretty much anything. I headed straight to the kitchen and opened the fridge, relishing the blast of cool air on my hot skin.

But on the glass shelf where my 2 percent milk always sits was a carton of oat milk. Behind it sat a large glass bottle of something called SouperFoods, which according to the label was a cold spinach, kale, and green apple soup that you drink like a smoothie.

The bathroom wasn't the only place Mr. Pembrook had taken over, unless my bacon-cheeseburger-loving mom had converted to veganism while I was away.

Mom walked in the kitchen with Mr. Pebbles right behind her. She put her palm to her forehead and said, "I'm so sorry I forgot to buy cow's milk!"

"Since when do you call real milk *cow's* milk?" I asked.

"Gavin introduced me to oat milk and I haven't had a sinus infection since. But I have everything we need for our *Gilmore Girls* marathon." Mom ticked her list off on her fingers: "Our Luke's Diner mugs, the makings for Luke's famous burgers and fries, and Pop Tarts, Mallomars, and Red Vines for dessert."

"Oh no. I forgot." I closed the fridge door. "I made plans. Can we do it tomorrow night?"

Mom tilted her head and stared at me, looking more perplexed than mad. "How could you forget our annual post-camp tradition? We do it every year."

"Maisy and I are hanging out with the M & Ms at Mia's house. Please, can I go?"

"Mia Atwater?" Two vertical lines appeared between Mom's eyes. "I thought you didn't like those girls because they're materialistic, fake, and superficial. Your words, not mine."

"I was just being judgmental last year because I had no friends. Besides, the M & Ms are the most popular girls in school. Why wouldn't I jump at the chance to hang out with them?"

"Since when do you care about being popular?" Mom asked.

"I don't want to be alone anymore. Being popular is the exact opposite of that," I said.

"But you have Maisy back," Mom said. "You're not alone anymore."

"Yeah and if the M & Ms don't accept me, I'll lose Maisy all over again."

"Maisy seems different. I don't think you have to worry about her leaving you behind again," Mom said.

"This is middle school, Mom. It's survival of the fittest, which in this case means hanging out with the M & Ms. So I need to make that happen, no matter what."

MAISY

"Isa's little, like us, but super tough. She doesn't let anyone push her around." I shouted so Grandma could hear me over the wind whipping around us in the Jeep.

Grandma sat in the back with me. She wore a bandanna tied around her hair to keep it from flying about and sticking to her lip gloss like mine was currently doing. "Isa sounds like a spark plug."

I nodded because being a spark plug is a huge compliment coming from Grandma. "We have to go on the Abercrombie site so I can show you some of Poppy's modeling pictures. She's the prettiest person I've ever met, but she never brags," I said.

"That's good." Grandma nodded. "No one likes a bragger."

"It should be easy to stay in touch with your camp friends during the school year since you guys all have cell phones," Dad said, as he turned into our driveway. "Not like when I was a kid and long distance was so expensive."

Grandma took off her seat belt and slowly climbed down from the car with Dad's help. "In my day, it was letter writing or nothing. I made a lot of friends at camp, but only stayed friends with the ones who actually wrote back."

"Sounds kind of harsh, Mom," Dad said.

Grandma smoothed down the front of her tunic and tugged her pant legs down. "I only stay friends with people who are willing to put in as much effort as I am. So if some girl tried to act like we were best friends after a whole school year of not writing . . . well, I wasn't having that."

"That's savage, Grandma," I said.

"That's my mom," Dad said. "Keeping it real since 1950."

"Fake friends are worse than fake handbags." Grandma smiled, like she was proud of herself. "I saw that on a meme."

Dad laughed. "I don't know what you did before Facebook."

I unhitched my seat belt and jumped down from the car as soon as I saw our front yard. "You fixed Mom's garden!"

When I was little, we had the best garden in town. Mom was so good at gardening that other women from town took pictures of our yard to give to their landscapers. When I left for camp, the most depressing sign of Mom's situation was her garden, which had become overgrown with weeds and filled with dead flowers.

"I'm not much of a gardener, but my friend Bernadette

volunteers at the Botanical Garden. We spent a lot of time Face-Timing while I cleaned things up," Grandma said.

Dad smiled from ear to ear. "It's been great having Grandma here. She really helped get the house in order."

Dad's voice was funny—like the car salesman who tried to upsell us the fancier minivan model with the moon roof. The front yard looked much better with the hot pink and purple flowering bushes by the front door, the rows of white, pink, and lavender flowers lining the house, and Mom's vegetable garden boxes full of tomatoes, zucchinis, eggplants, and all different kinds of lettuce. But that tingly feeling was back in my fingers.

Grandma smiled at me. "After all these years working, I thought I was going to be bored. But I have to admit, I've enjoyed fixing up the house."

"I'm so excited to get back to my room! After bunking with four girls all summer, I can't wait to sleep in my own bed without anyone else snoring or talking." I walked to the front door and waited for Dad to unlock it. "My camp friends are great, but they don't believe in personal space."

Dad and Grandma looked at each other.

Now on top of tingly hands and feet, my heart was pounding. The worst thing you can do to an anxious person is dangle a secret in front of them.

"Will someone *please* tell me what's going on?" I demanded.

Dad cleared his throat. "Grandma's staying with us to help out while Mom's in treatment."

Grandma added, "And to help make the transition easier when your mom comes home."

"When is Mom—" I started to ask, but Dad cut me off.

"After you left for camp, I realized how much you were doing around the house to cover for Mom." Dad put his hand on my shoulder. "I figured out you were the one ordering groceries, making Addy's gym food, cleaning up, and doing laundry. With Grandma here, you can focus on yourself."

I looked at Grandma. "You didn't have to retire early. I could've taken care of everything, like I always do."

Grandma smiled at me, but her eyes looked sad. "The only thing you should be taking care of is yourself."

It was getting awkward crowding around the front step together, while we all waited for Dad to let us in. "But Mom's coming home soon, and everything will go back to normal. Right, Dad?"

Dad cleared his throat. "We still don't know when Mom's coming home. But when she does, we want to make things as stress-free as possible for her."

I wasn't sure how Grandma staying with us was going to make things stress-free for Mom since usually Mom hated Grandma "looking over her shoulder." Mom says Grandma loves to remind everyone that she taught full-time, while raising Dad and his brother, Jerry, on her own after her husband died. One time I heard Grandma on the phone saying to her friend Bernadette, "How can someone who hasn't worked for the past decade be so stressed out? What could possibly be that hard about her life? Stressed out is clipping coupons so you can afford Wonder Bread and bologna."

Grandma smoothed down her thick black hair so it looked as perfect as always. "And we want to make things easy for you and Addy."

"If things are going to be so much easier, why're you guys acting so weird?" I asked. "It's like you haven't told me *everything*."

Dad chewed on his bottom lip. "Well, Grandma living with us is probably going to be a long-term thing. And she has to sleep somewhere, so . . ."

"I stole your room, kiddo," Grandma cut in.

"What?! Where will I sleep?"

There was no way I was sharing my room with Grandma.

"You're bunking with Addy," Dad said.

"What?" I yelled.

"You will be sharing a room with your sister," he said, slower this time.

"This can't be happening," I said, my heart pounding faster. I backed away from them.

"Maisy," they both said.

But I couldn't hear another word. "You're ruining my life!" I screamed before storming into the house.

I headed straight for my room and opened the door, hoping this was all just some big misunderstanding. But there was no mistake. My room wasn't my room anymore.

My blanket set was gone, and Grandma's ruffled white quilt from her house in the Berkshires was tucked into my mattress. Every part of me was erased from the room, including my tapestry, my photo collages, and my table full of beauty products. It even smelled different in there, like Grandma's Shalimar perfume.

This can't be happening. This can't be happening.

Dad and Grandma finally made it up the stairs.

"You're going to love your new room," said Dad. "Grandma helped me redecorate."

I let out a big breath. "New stuff isn't gonna make up for me sharing a room with my little sister."

Grandma smoothed down my hair. "Addy's at the gym so much, you'll have the room to yourself most of the time. Come see it. Your dad worked really hard to make things nice for you girls."

Dad grabbed my hand and pulled me down the hall. "Come on, Mini. You're going to love it."

I held my breath while Dad opened the door. Addy's room used to be hot pink with a bright purple accent wall that was covered floor to ceiling with stuffed animals and gymnastics posters. Now, it was decorated in shades of blush, cream, and gold. It was like someone used an Instagram filter on the room.

Each side of the room had a white loft bed with a desk, chair, and bookshelf set underneath. The beds were covered with gold and cream bedding that matched the fluffy carpet. I had to readjust my face so Dad couldn't tell how awesome I thought it was. I could take some really artsy pics in there and the loft bed looked cozy with all the new throw pillows. It really would be the perfect room . . . if I didn't have to share it with my little sister.

>--· CHAPTER FOUR ·--<

BEA

"ARE YOU SURE IT'S OKAY IF I GO OUT?" I ASKED MOM, WITH ONE hand on the door handle. Part of me wanted to snuggle up on the couch binge-watching *Gilmore Girls* with her and Mr. Pebbles, but I knew an M & M would always choose her friends over a night at home with her mom.

"Of course." Mom smiled. "I just want you to be happy this year."

I ran over and hugged her. "I really missed you, even though it doesn't look that way."

Mom laughed. "I missed you, too. Don't forget your bike helmet."

I was just clipping my helmet on over my mounds of frizzy hair when I saw a silver Prius snake down our street. He wasn't wearing a bowtie, but I was certain the hipster driving the eco-friendly car was none other than Mr. Pembrook. No wonder Mom didn't seem that upset about missing our annual *Gilmore Girls* fest.

I used my foot to scoot out of the driveway as fast as I could. As I pedaled toward Maisy's house, I wondered how long it had taken Mom to call Mr. Pembrook.

When I got there, she was waiting for me on her front lawn. "Hurry up! We need to start your makeover. It's going to take a while."

I leaned my bike behind the garage and smirked. "Real subtle."

"I swear I didn't mean it like that." Maisy put her hand over her mouth. "We need time for the keratin treatment."

"The what?" I asked. As much as I hated my unruly curls, I never thought about getting rid of them permanently.

"I convinced my grandma to pick up a kit for us, and I watched, like, a million YouTube tutorials," Maisy said, as she walked into her house.

"Are you sure you know what you're doing? Because I have enough problems without my hair falling out." I followed her up the stairs.

"You think you have problems? My grandma moved in with us and stole my room. Now, I'm stuck sharing a room with Addy," Maisy said, as she opened Addy's door.

I gasped as soon as I walked in. "It looks like . . ." I started.

"Page forty-three of the Pottery Barn Teen catalog." Maisy held up the catalog centerfold.

Maisy's dad had duplicated everything, from the white beadboard loft beds with desk nooks underneath to the duvet covers. He had even bought the matching throw pillows in shades of pale pink and gold. Each half of the room was a mirror image of the other, except one side had a large metal letter A strung with fairy lights over the bed, and the wall was covered with framed pictures of Addy in her competition leotard flying through the air or flipping on the bars. Maisy's side was demarcated with a metal M on the wall with photos of Maisy hanging out with the M & Ms, a picture of her playing guitar on stage at the school talent show, and a collage of pictures from all of the plays and musicals she had starred in over the years.

Meanwhile, Mom and I hadn't gotten around to taking down my old Hello Kitty wallpaper border, and my idea of bed chic was a matching set of sheets from Target.

"You're so lucky," I said. "This room is amazing!"

Maisy sighed. "I have to share it with my younger sister."

"She's not home that much. Besides, I would give anything to have a sister to share a room with," I said. "And before you say anything, Peyton and Vivi don't count."

"You can have mine," Maisy said. "Let's get started on your hair."

Maisy had been right about the keratin treatment taking hours. Between washing, applying the awful-smelling cream that made my eyes water, blow-drying, and flat-ironing, by the end, my neck and shoulders were tight and my scalp was sore, but when I ran my hand down my hair, it felt like a smooth silk sheet. My tight curls and frizz had been stretched out into shiny locks of hair that were twice as long as usual. Even the color looked different. Normally, my red hair was twisted into such tight ringlets, it looked like a big orange blob. With my hair glossy and straight, you could see all the gradient shades from strawberry blond to honey to auburn. For the first time in my life, I actually liked my red hair.

I stood in front of Maisy's mirror and couldn't believe who I saw staring back at me. "I look like a completely different person."

I tried to cover my face with as much hair as I could. "If only you could wave a magic wand and make my freckles disappear," I said.

Maisy tossed me a makeup bag. "I raided Mom's makeup stash. She's almost as pale as you, so the concealer should match."

I pulled out a glass bottle of creamy ivory foundation that looked and smelled exponentially more expensive than the Cover Girl my mom wore. I held it up to my arm. "Perfect."

Maisy pulled out a tray of brushes, foam triangles, and pointed Q-tips. "Let's get to work."

With one stroke of foundation, the freckles across the bridge of my nose disappeared. I leaned forward to get a better look. "My freckles are gone! You're a magician!"

"Wait till I'm really done," Maisy said with a grin.

After swiping, blending, highlighting, and contouring, Maisy had covered every last freckle and added angles where I didn't have any. She used a light brown pencil to shade in my practically invisible eyebrows, then she added brown mascara to my eyelashes, which, unfortunately, are as invisible as my brows. Last, she applied a shiny nude lip gloss.

I teared up when I looked in the mirror. It was like the real me was finally on the outside where everyone could see.

Maisy pushed me toward the bathroom. "I laid out a bathing suit and outfit. Go try it on."

I walked into Addy and Maisy's Ballet Slipper Pink bathroom. It still smelled like fresh paint, and everything was new, from the fluffy pale gold towels to the white Egyptian cotton shower curtain. It was obvious Dr. Winters had put a lot of work into making over the room for the girls. Meanwhile, my room at Dad's new house consisted of a pullout couch next to the washer and dryer in the basement.

I pulled on the navy blue bikini top which had just enough ruffle to give the illusion of curves. The simple navy bottoms fit perfectly, and Maisy had laid out matching navy flip-flops and a white flowy sundress to pull the outfit together.

I put on the clothes and smoothed my hair again. I had spent my entire life walking past mirrors without even a glance at my reflection, and now I couldn't stop looking at myself.

I ran in the room and twirled around like a princess.

Maisy put her hand on her chest and breathed in. "OMG! You look amazing!"

I ran my hands down my new, sleek hair. "I feel like a new person."

I waited for Maisy to join in on my excitement, but she was uncharacteristically quiet for long enough to make me uncomfortable. I cleared my throat. "Why are you looking at me like that?"

Maisy sighed. "This is just a little taste of how hard you're gonna have to work to get in with the M & Ms."

MAISY

I pulled on a pair of jean shorts over my bathing suit and slipped on flip-flops. "Let's go, Bea."

"I'll be right down," Bea said, leaning in closer to the mirror. "I need to touch up my lip gloss."

As I headed downstairs by myself, I realized I was kind of missing the old Bea already.

"Wait! Where are you girls going? I'm cooking dinner." Grandma bustled out from the kitchen wearing Dad's King of the Grill apron. It hung all the way down to her feet, and the strings were wrapped around her waist a bunch of times. "Your favorite! Lasagna."

Stouffer's frozen lasagna is definitely not my favorite food, but compared to the other things Grandma makes, like tuna casserole with corn flake crust, ketchup-glazed meatloaf, and mashed potatoes that come from a box, it's not so bad. Grandma's family came here from the Philippines when she was five and her mom thought all of the packaged food we have in America was a treat. Pretty much all our recipes from Dad's side of the family come from the back of a can or a box.

I twisted my face into a sad face. "Sorry, Grandma. We're going to Mia's."

Grandma folded her arms across her chest and sighed. "But I just preheated the oven."

"Save me a piece," I said, hoping there wouldn't be any left by the time I got home.

Bea flipped her shiny hair over her shoulder as she walked down the stairs. "Hi, Mrs. Winters."

Grandma's eyes grew wide and she threw her hands in the air. "Wow! You look beautiful, Bea!"

"Thank you. Maisy gave me a makeover."

"You looked great before, but a little hair and makeup never hurts." Grandma smoothed down her own hair, which she had trimmed every six weeks so it was always the exact same length. "I'll never forget the first time I wore lipstick. It was called Cherries in the Snow."

Bea asked in a dreamy voice, "Didn't it feel amazing the first time you put it on?"

Grandma smirked. "Yes, it did. Until my father got home from work and scrubbed my face with a washcloth."

I made a polite laugh, because I had already heard this story a million times. "We have to go, Grandma."

Grandma fired questions at us without taking a breath. "Where does Mia live? How are you getting there? When will you be back? Will her mom be home?"

"Mia lives in the big house at the entrance to Red Maple Corners," I said. "It's only two blocks away and I always bike there."

Grandma wagged a finger at us. "Make sure you both wear helmets and stay on the sidewalk. I don't care what anyone says, no one should be riding a bicycle in the road with all those cars. People drive like maniacs in this town. All these moms always rushing their kids to this practice or that lesson."

"Okay, Grandma," I said, with my hand on the door handle.

"Not so fast." Grandma shook her finger at me again. "You didn't answer my question. Will her mom be there?"

"Yes," I said, not mentioning that Mia's mom believed in giving her space to hang out with her friends. So even when she was home, we pretty much had the backyard and rec room to ourselves.

"Text me when you get there," Grandma said. "And be home before dark."

I turned the doorknob. "Okay."

I opened the garage and wheeled my bike out from behind Dad's Jeep. "For the past year, no one knew where I was or when I was coming back. You'd think Grandma would trust me to go down the street to Mia's house."

"Maybe I should skip the helmet," Bea said, holding her helmet inches over her head. "It'll ruin my hair."

"Perfect hair won't matter if you get hit by a car and your brains are all over the road," I said. "Wear the helmet."

Bea pulled it on as carefully as possible. "What if I get sweaty on the ride and my hair starts to curl up?"

I climbed on my bike and said, "The ride's short. You won't have enough time to get sweaty."

Bea started blinking fast. "What if they look at me and all they see is the old Bea?"

"There was nothing wrong with the old Bea," I said.

But I knew she didn't believe me.

CHAPTER FIVE

BEA

I KNEW I WAS OUT OF MY LEAGUE AS SOON AS WE BIKED THROUGH the wrought iron gates into Red Maple Corners. I had never been to Mia's house before, but it felt like I had because people always posted pictures from there. I knew there was an oversized rec room with an air hockey table, foosball table, and a huge flat screen set up for marathon video game sessions. The main attraction was her in-ground pool that looked like it belonged in a resort, with its diving board and slide, waterfalls, and bubbling Jacuzzi.

"Come on. I can hear the girls in the back," Maisy said.

We left our bikes on the front lawn because apparently one of the benefits of living behind a gate is not having to lock your bike up.

We walked to the side of the house and stopped at the wooden gate that led to the pool. The sound of girls shrieking and laughing carried over the fence. It sounded like my bunkmates clowning around at the lake. At first, I felt reassured, like maybe these girls weren't going to be that different from my camp friends. Then I thought about all the times they had walked past me in the halls at school as if they could see right through me.

Maisy had her game face on, the same expression she had made right before she climbed the ropes course and brought us to our Amelia Cup win. "I'll go first. Come into the yard when I say our code word."

"Wait!" I grabbed Maisy's wrist. "What's the code word?"

"Genius Whisperer." She winked at me. "Obviously."

As Maisy headed toward the back, I peeked over the gate and saw that Mia's Instagram pictures hadn't done it justice. The enormous pool was filled with oversized inflatable swans, unicorns, and donuts. The grass was as green as the football turf at school and every single blade looked like it was the exact same length. I wondered if the gardener carried a ruler when he trimmed the grass. There was a full-scale outdoor kitchen, with a high-end barbeque and a brick oven that smelled like it had pizza cooking in it.

You could hear the girls laughing and shrieking over the music that pumped from speakers built into the rocks surrounding the pool. We were definitely in popular-girl territory.

I wish I had Maisy's confidence. She walked right into Mia's yard as if she were at her own house and shouted, "Hey, girls! Look who's back!"

Madison hopped off the donut float where she had been laying out with Chloe, pulled herself out of the pool, ran to Maisy, and wrapped her in a water-logged hug.

"OMG! Maisy!" she squealed. "Missed you!"

"Missed you more!" Maisy cried.

While Madison and Maisy competed about who missed who more, Chloe sat on the float alone. I could see the struggle written all over her face. She was new to the group, added while Maisy was gone. It was obvious she didn't know what to do with herself without Madison attached to her hip. I knew what it was like to be in the world with everyone else but to still feel all alone.

When the girls finally stopped squealing, Maisy said, "You guys! I brought a present from camp. Our Genius Whisperer!"

I took a deep breath, smoothed down my hair, and adjusted my sunglasses before walking down the stone path to the pool area. This was it. The moment that would guarantee me entrée into the M & Ms or seal my fate as a middle school reject.

Time slowed to a crawl. I stepped onto the manicured lawn. The only sound was the water flowing over the rock fountain into the pool and my flip-flops slapping against the bottoms of my feet as I walked toward the M & Ms.

No one said a word. They all stared at me with blank looks. It's not like I expected them to give me the same welcome they had given Maisy, but I didn't know what to do with their silence. I looked at Maisy, but she looked just as confused as I was.

Finally, Mia stepped forward.

She said, "Hi, I'm Mia," with a little half wave.

I froze because I knew exactly who Mia was. She was the first person to break the principal's cardinal rule about inviting all the girls from class to her birthday party last year. Her mother had argued that the final year of elementary school was the optimal time to learn how to cope with the harsh realities of social hierarchy. Needless to say, I hadn't been invited to that party.

Supermodel-tall Meghan leaned down to my paltry average height. "You look so familiar. Were we on swim team together at the club a couple years back?"

Madison shook her head. "That was Will Flanagan's cousin who was visiting from Ireland."

I had known Madison and Meghan since day care. How could one year of invisibility erase my entire identity?

Maisy laughed a little too loud. "Clark Rutner isn't the only Glow Up of the Year. You guys, this is Bea."

Mia leaned in closer and ran her palm over my hair. "O...M...G! Bea Thompson? Is that you under those sunglasses and amazing hair?"

I took a deep breath, then pushed the sunglasses on top of my head. Next thing I knew, I was surrounded by all the girls touching my hair and oohing and aahing like I was a new puppy.

"What salon did you go to? I've been begging my mom for a keratin treatment," said Meghan, whose hair is admittedly a little prone to frizz, but nothing a little flat-ironing can't control. She was also blessed with the perfect amount of freckles, dainty little ones sprinkled across the bridge of her nose and cheeks, unlike mine that merged into melanin blobs with the slightest bit of sun exposure.

"Our camp counselor did it. She's in college, but she and Bea are like this." Maisy folded her middle finger over her pointer.

Mia couldn't stop petting my hair. "That's so cool."

"Totally cool," Madison said.

Madison is average height, and her limp brown hair hangs down on both sides of her forehead, not too long, not too short. Her appearance fits her role as mouse of the group, the one who was always angling to keep her spot even though she had been friends with these girls her whole life.

"Yeah, so cool," mumbled Chloe, who was clearly looking to Madison for her every move. She was even wearing the same exact bathing suit as Madison, with white nautical rope tied up the sides, but in red rather than blue.

Mia ran her index finger across my cheekbone. "Where did your freckles go?"

"Good foundation can fix anything," Maisy said.

"You know Clark?" asked Madeline.

"We're in all the same classes," I said.

"And don't forget Robotics Club," Maisy piped in.

Madeline narrowed her eyes at me. She was the smartest of all the M & Ms. If anyone was going to bust us, it was Madeline.

"Penelope Green's in all the same classes with Todd Montgomery, but that doesn't mean he would actually talk to her," she said.

Mia nodded. "Agreed."

"Bea, send him a Snap," Maisy said.

That sounded much easier than it actually was. I hadn't used Snapchat since Maisy and I stopped being friends. As soon as I opened the app on my phone, I was lost. I stared at the screen, willing it to tell me what to do.

Maisy grabbed my phone. "This new stupid iPhone update is literally the worst. It kept freezing up Bea's phone on the way home from camp."

Meghan scratched at a mosquito bite on one of her impossibly long legs. "I'm terrified of updates. I keep ignoring the reminders."

Madeline grimaced. "Your phone's gonna crash."

Meanwhile, Maisy slid her finger across my screen, got it set up to Snap Clark, and handed it back to me.

I shot her a look of gratitude before taking a selfie and adding the caption, *Signed up for robotics!*

Madeline grabbed my phone right out of my hand. "Why don't you have anyone on your Snapchat feed?"

I shrugged, easing myself into this new role where I told lie after lie to stay afloat. "That update completely cleared my feed."

"See, guys! This is why I never update," Meghan said.

I said a silent prayer to the tech gods that Meghan's phone wouldn't crash because of me.

My phone pinged. I opened up a picture of Clark standing on his diving board with the sun shining on his blond highlights. The message read, *Like the new hair,* across his golden abs.

"Whoa!" Meghan held up both of her hands. "He really is the Glow Up of the Year."

"And Bea really is our Genius Whisperer," Mia said.

MAISY

Last summer, I hated being around Mom. I never knew how she was going to act or what kind of mood she was going to be in. Dad was always at work, Addy was always at the gym, and Bea was away for six weeks at Camp Amelia, which left me stuck with Mom by myself.

I rode my bike to the Mapleton Country Club every morning as soon as it opened. I watched the pool moms spray down their kids with sunscreen, help them with their goggles, and feed them snacks.

I would set up my towel near one of the normal families and imagine I was going home with them at the end of the day. I used to have *that* mom, but I didn't know if I would ever get her back.

I stayed at the club every day until Dad texted me that he was on his way home from work. It didn't matter that I couldn't swim, or that I had no one to hang out with while Bea was at camp. The only thing I cared about was getting as far away from Mom as possible.

Then, one day Madison, walking past me at the pool, asked me where I got my bathing suit. Next thing I knew, I was hanging out with the M & Ms at their spot near the snack bar. We spent hours taking selfies, looking at back-to-school clothes online, and scrolling Instagram while we ate ketchup-drenched fries, greasy grilled cheeses, and icy slushies. I finally stopped thinking about Mom every second of the day.

Bea was sitting on the edge of the diving board with Madeline, who was adding all of the Snapchat contacts she thought Bea lost in her imaginary phone update.

"Don't forget your sunblock!" I called.

"OMG! You sound like my mother," Madison said, in a snarky tone.

Chloe tilted her head back and laughed, like Madison just said the funniest thing ever.

I don't know what annoyed me more, that Chloe had stolen the spot I had carved out for Bea or that she followed Madison around, copying everything she did and said. She looked so desperate, and it made me worry that I had looked the exact same way when I started hanging out with the M & Ms last summer.

"Maisy was the sunblock police at camp," Bea said, for the second time that day. Only this time she didn't say it like it was a good thing.

As much as I wanted to sass Bea back, I held it in. Bea forgave me for being a huge jerk last year, and now it was my turn to be the bigger person. Madison, on the other hand, was being annoying. She thought she was so cool just because Chloe was following her around.

"Toss me some of that sunblock, Maisy," Madeline said. "I bet you girls didn't know black girls can burn."

I walked over to Madeline and handed her the sunblock since I have really bad aim.

"Snap Clark again, Bea," Madeline said. "Hopefully he'll send another bathing suit pic."

Bea smoothed her hair down and sat up straight on the diving board. She sucked in her cheeks, making her lips all pouty, and took a selfie. For someone who didn't know how to use Snapchat half an hour ago, she was really getting into it.

Two seconds later she held up her phone. "He Snapped back."

Mia ran over. "Show us!"

We all crowded around Bea's phone.

"Is he seriously reading on one of the last days of summer vacation?" Meghan asked.

"But he's so cute doing it," Madeline said with a sigh.

"Does it really matter what he's doing?" Bea asked. "He's shirtless."

Bea had picked up the M & Ms' language just as quickly as she had learned Spanish in first grade.

Clark held up a book with a bright yellow cover that said *Steel Trap: A How-to Book for Humans Trying to Make It in the Robotics World.*

Madison leaned over Bea's shoulder. "Um . . . What does that even mean?"

"Yeah, what does that mean?" Chloe echoed.

Bea took a selfie with a thumbs-up and captioned it, *Tim Landon is goals!*

Madeline stared at Bea. "Who is Tim Landon and why is he goals?"

"Tim Landon's the next Steve Jobs. This is the summer pick for his book club," Bea said.

Mia laughed. "Good call on the Genius Whisperer, Maisy."

"Yeah, good call," Madison said.

My phone vibrated against my leg. I picked it up and almost dropped it when I saw who was texting me.

From: Mom
To: Maisy

Earned phone privileges. You don't have to text back. Just wanted to let you know I'm here if you want to talk.

I held my breath as the little dots showed up like Mom was texting more, but then they disappeared. My head starting buzzing like it was filled with seltzer bubbles.

"I need to go," I mumbled to Bea, not loud enough for the other girls to hear.

Bea's phone pinged. "OMG, you guys! How cute is this?"

The girls crowded around Bea's phone and drooled over a picture of Clark cuddling with a fluffy little white dog.

"Does it get any cuter?" yelled Madeline.

"I know!" Bea shrieked. Then she turned to me. "Did you say something, Maisy?"

I swallowed hard. "Don't worry about it," I said.

But I don't think she heard me.

→··· CHAPTER SIX ···←

BEA

A COUPLE OF HOURS LATER, MAISY AND I CLIMBED OFF A GIGANTIC inflatable pizza slice. We didn't even need to towel off because we had stuck to our mission not to actually get wet in the pool.

"We have to go," Maisy said, while she pulled on her jean shorts. "My grandma's staying with us and she's super annoying."

Mia called out from her perch on the unicorn float, "We're all wearing red the first day."

"It's a power color." Madeline looked up from her phone. "I read about it on Snapchat."

"It's going to be our signature color this year," Meghan said.

"But it has to be *Poppy* Red," Mia added.

I couldn't tell if this directive was aimed at me or just Maisy, so while Maisy nodded, I jutted my chin up the tiniest bit so that it could be interpreted as a nod or a tic.

"Byeeee!" called the girls in unison, as Maisy and I opened the gate.

"Byeeee!" Maisy called back. I joined in on the tail end of the "eeeee" so that I didn't sound too desperate.

As soon as we pedaled our bikes down the driveway, I asked, "Do I wear red on the first day or is that too presumptuous? But if I don't wear it and the offer was actually for me too, then won't it look like I don't want to be part of the group?"

Maisy's voice was dull. "Yes."

"To which part?" I asked.

Maisy made a sharp right out of Mia's driveway and mumbled, "Wear red."

Maisy took off so fast I had to pump my legs to catch up to her. "But are you just saying that as a strategy to push my way into the group? Or do you think Mia was actually including me?"

"Stop overthinking everything," Maisy snapped.

I pedaled harder to get in front of her and then I planted my bike across the sidewalk so she was trapped. "What's going on with you?" I asked.

Maisy sighed. "What're you talking about?"

"This is usually the moment when you brag about your plan," I said. "Which, I have to admit, is pretty amazing."

Maisy loosened the strap under her helmet. "I'm tired. Just this morning we were at Camp Amelia."

I scooted my bike closer to hers. "Now that we're back in Mapleton, you're going to start hiding things again? Isn't that how we got into this mess in the first place?"

Maisy's eyes grew wide. "How'd you know?"

"You've been really quiet for the last hour. What happened?" I asked.

Maisy pulled her phone out of her bike basket and handed it to me.

She looked down at the ground while I read the text from her mom.

"Are you going to text back?" I asked.

Maisy took her phone back. "So she can think everything's okay? It's her fault I have to share a room with Addy and that Grandma's all up in my business."

"You're going to have to talk to her eventually," I said. "Like when she comes home."

"I'm not talking to her until I have to, and she's not coming home for a while," Maisy said. "Let's go before Grandma sends the police looking for us."

"No more secrets, okay?" I said. "I can't help you if you don't tell me what's going on."

Maisy took off toward her house without answering. She didn't even wave goodbye when I turned off on my street.

As I got closer to my house, I saw a gray Prius pulling out of the driveway. I wiped away the image of Mr. Pembrook hanging out with Mom while I was gone. I couldn't wait to show Mom my makeover.

Mom and Mr. Pebbles were waiting for me on the living room couch. I walked into the room and twirled around so they could get the full effect of the new me.

Mom ran over to me, her eyes welling up with tears. "What did you do to your curls?"

She ran her hands from the crown of my head to the ends of my hair. It felt completely different from when the M & Ms were petting my hair and saying how beautiful it was.

"You don't like it?" I heard my voice soar an octave higher.

Mom's own curls bounced with emphasis as she said, "I love your curls. They're part of you."

"It only lasts three months," I said.

"Three months!" Mom cried. "And since when do you wear makeup?"

"You always tell me to do things that make me feel good about myself." I waved my hands over my face and hair. "This makes me feel good."

She sighed. "It's not that I don't like your new look, Bea. I just have to get used to it."

"I know you always liked us having our big curly hair together," I said.

Mom put her hands on my cheeks and lifted my face till I made eye contact with her. "Bea, you're your own person. You don't need to look like me or *anybody* else. Got it?"

"But if *you* want to look like *me,* we can always ask Maisy to give you a keratin treatment," I said.

She smirked. "Very funny."

My phone beeped. "Mom, look! I'm in the group text with the rest of the M & Ms!"

From: Mia

To: Maisy, Madeline, Meghan, Madison, Chloe, Genius Whisperer

Flag pole @ 7:25 Monday. Check Seventeen's Insta story for POPPY RED looks.

Mom raised her eyebrow. "I'm assuming you're the Genius Whisperer?"

"I have a nickname and everything!" I practically squealed.

"But what does it mean?" Mom asked.

"Long story. Can you take Maisy and me to the mall tomorrow?"

Mom paused for a minute like she wanted to say something deep, but then she just smiled. "Of course. We won't leave till we find some cute Poppy Red outfits."

MAISY

As soon as I wheeled my bike into the garage, Addy came running out of the house like a maniac. She threw herself into me and squeezed so hard, I felt like she was breaking my ribs. Even though she's two years younger than me, and a couple of inches shorter, Addy probably weighs about twenty pounds more and it's all rock-solid muscle. Dad always says lifting Addy is like picking up a bag of boulders.

"Addy! You're breaking me!" I yelled.

Addy laughed and let go. "I forgot how wimpy you are."

I pointed to myself. "I'm a normal person. You're just used to hanging out with superhumans."

"True." Addy pulled herself into a handstand and walked across the lawn on her hands.

"Can you believe Grandma moved in?" I hissed when she teetered near me. "And now we have to share a room?"

Addy spent so much of her life upside down that talking while walking on her hands was no big deal to her. "Isn't it awesome? It's going to be like a sleepover every night!"

"Just don't leave any of your sweaty leotards on my half of the room," I said.

"Whatever." Addy flipped back to her feet and pulled her phone out of the top of her leotard. She smiled as her fingers flew across her phone screen.

"Who're you texting?" I asked.

Addy looked up from the phone. "Why are you all up in my business?"

"That better not be Mom," I said, reaching for her phone. But Addy had a death grip on it.

"Why do you care?" she asked.

"The last time we saw her she almost drove the minivan off the Maple Creek Bridge—with us in it. And you're texting her with heart emojis like nothing happened."

"I didn't use heart emojis," Addy said, as her phone lit up with another text.

I leaned over her shoulder. "Kissy face emojis. Same thing."

"Are you gonna stay mad at Mom forever?" Addy asked.

I twisted my hair into a bun. "Dr. Beth says everyone has their own timeline for forgiveness."

Addy folded her arms across her muscular chest. "I won't bug you about your timeline if you stop being so bossy about mine."

"Why do you have to be so annoying?" I asked.

She popped into a handstand and walked toward the front steps with as much attitude as possible while being upside down.

I sighed. It was really hard to stay annoyed at someone who's so happy and bouncy all the time. "Fine. Whatever."

Grandma opened the front door. "Addy, stay like that so I can video you for Facebook."

I rolled my eyes.

Grandma focused her phone on Addy. Of course Addy had to show off. She didn't just walk up the stairs on her hands, she did a push-up on each step.

Grandma leaned into the phone and spoke like it was a microphone. "Watch out for my granddaughter, Addy. This little firecracker's gonna be in the Olympics one day."

Grandma turned the phone toward me. "There's my other granddaughter, Maisy."

I smiled without showing any teeth and gave a half wave.

The rest of the night didn't get any better. I had to share a closet with Addy, and even though Dad had put up a divider in the middle, just looking at her half made me anxious. All the hangers were pointing in different directions and the clothes were all hanging by a thread, ready to fall on the floor at any second. I spent an hour fixing up her half of the closet before I even got started putting away my camp clothes.

For dinner, Grandma reheated the Stouffer's lasagna in the microwave so the edges of the pasta were hard and the sauce tasted like metal. Grandma doesn't care that microwaves creep me out, ever since I read that they use radiation to cook the food. I also had to drink a big glass of whole milk with Ovaltine powder in it at dinner because Grandma thinks I'm too skinny. The milk tasted like Whoppers, which are seriously the worst candy ever. When I finally got to bed, I had to watch gymnastics videos with Addy on YouTube when all I wanted to do was go to sleep. Who would have ever thought I would actually miss being at camp?

When Grandma turned on the light at seven the next morning, I groaned. "But it's my last morning to sleep in."

She climbed up the loft ladder and pulled my comforter back. "If you don't get up now, you'll never fall asleep tonight. Time to reset your body clock for the school year."

"Ugh." I pulled my comforter back over my face.

"Breakfast's in five," Grandma said.

"K," Addy practically sang as she jumped down off her loft bed with a loud thump. Then she ran to the bathroom and made as much noise as humanly possible. She is seriously the loudest teeth brusher in the world.

Five minutes later, I was sitting at the kitchen table with my eyes half closed. Addy came bouncing into the room wearing a blue sparkly leotard and a pair of black spandex shorts. She threw on a gray Five Rivers Gymnastics hoodie over her head and started pulling her hair back in a tight ponytail.

Grandma handed her a slimy green smoothie. "Hold this so I can get a pic. I want to show my Facebook friends the dedication it takes to train."

Addy held up her drink with one hand and rested the other hand on her hip. She gave Grandma a big, cheesy smile, like she was in an actual commercial.

Grandma muttered out loud while she typed. "No Lucky Charms for this girl! #greenjuice #olympicbound #gymnastics-grandma #proudgranny."

I rolled my eyes. "It's too early for this."

"Don't worry," said Grandma. "I made you a Lender's."

One of the best parts of living in New York is the bagels. I literally dreamed about a big, fluffy-on-the-inside, crunchy-on-the-outside bagel while I was stuck in the middle of nowhere at Camp Amelia. Grandma is the only New Yorker I know who buys frozen bagels.

Addy chugged her green drink like it was a chocolate milkshake, which made me shudder.

I rubbed my upper lip. "You have a little something."

She wiped off her green mustache with the back of her hand. "I'm so excited about homeschooling. I mean gym schooling."

"Aren't you going to miss seeing everyone at school?" I asked.

Addy shrugged. "Nah. I have Tashie and Sage."

Grandma wagged a finger at her. "Don't forget they're your competition."

Addy slurped back more smoothie. "Just because they're my besties doesn't mean I would let them beat me."

Grandma gave her a fist bump; Addy had taught her how to do it yesterday. "That's right, Cookie."

Dad walked into the kitchen wearing a gray-and-white checkered shirt with black pinstriped pants, a black belt, and brown shoes and said, "Hi, girls."

"Dad, you can't wear that to work. Your residents are totally gonna rip on you," I said.

"What's wrong with this outfit?" Dad smoothed down his shirt. "I was going for the opposite of too matchy-matchy."

"I'll be right back," I said, scraping my chair back.

I ran upstairs to Dad's closet and grabbed a plain white button-down and a pair of black shoes that didn't look too scuffed up. I didn't want to think about the terrible outfits Dad had worn to work all summer without me home to keep an eye on him. Good thing he wore a white lab coat most of the day.

I ran downstairs two at a time but froze when I heard Addy ask, "When's Mom coming home?"

I held my breath.

"Soon. She can't wait to get back to you girls," Dad said.

Addy started to sound kind of panicky. "Will she be back in time for my first level-nine meet?"

"When is it?" Dad asked.

"Beginning of November," Addy said. "Coach Tracy wants me to jump right up to level ten after the first level-nine meet. But

I need to get eight point fives on all of my events and a thirty-four all around to qualify."

There was no way Mom would be ready to come home by November, and even if she thought she was, I wouldn't be ready to see her by then. My stomach started doing somersaults and I could feel beads of sweat popping up on my forehead.

"You're going to nail this meet," Grandma said. "You looked great at practice yesterday. That bar routine is really something."

"If I don't make level ten now, I won't have enough time to qualify for Junior Elite by the end of the season," Addy said. "I really need Mom there."

"Hopefully, she'll be home in time," Dad said. "But you're going to kick butt at that meet whether Mom's there or not. I know she will try her best to be there for you."

"Maisy! Your father's going to be late," Grandma yelled.

I took a deep breath and held it in for five counts. Then I breathed out for five. The flip-floppy feeling in my stomach was still there, but I didn't want Grandma to start yelling again, so I walked in and handed Dad the clothes.

He smiled. "Thanks, Mini. You saved me from being humiliated at work today."

I sat back down at the table and pushed the wannabe bagel away from me.

Dad took off the checkered shirt and threw it on the back of a chair. Then he pulled on the new shirt and buttoned it in record time.

I scooted my chair back. "Can I have a ride to Bea's?"

"What about your breakfast?" Grandma asked.

"Not hungry," I said.

Grandma shook her finger at me. "How do you expect to fatten up if you skip meals?"

I sighed. "I'll eat at Bea's."

Dad filled his travel mug with coffee. "Are they even awake yet?"

"Yes," I said. "We're going back-to-school shopping."

Dad looked at his watch. "You've got five minutes, so hurry up and get ready."

For once Dad didn't have to remind me to hurry. I wanted to get out of our house as quickly as possible.

CHAPTER SEVEN

BEA

MOM DOES ALL HER SHOPPING ONLINE. SHE KNOWS THE UPS GUY so well, she was invited to his wife's baby shower. Spending eight hours at the mall helping Maisy and me find every last Poppy Red article of clothing was clearly Mom's way of making up for her reaction to my makeover.

The next morning, as I was shoving my lunch pouch in my backpack, Maisy walked in the back door without knocking, like she had done practically all our lives, minus last year when we weren't friends.

"Is this too much?" I asked, pressing my hands down on the red T-shirt dress Maisy and Mom had convinced me to buy. "I feel like it's too much."

Mom lowered her head practically in her bowl of granola and oat milk. "Please tell Bea how awesome she looks. I only told her about twenty-five times, but I'm not getting anywhere."

"You look sooooo good, Bea!" Maisy said.

But when I took in Maisy's simple white denim shorts, Poppy Red boatneck tee, and navy sneakers, I knew I should've gone with a statement piece. I needed to blend in, not stand out like a big red tomato.

"Maybe I should change. This dress clashes with my hair," I said.

"Don't I tell you when you forget to brush the back of your hair? Or when you think you wrote an amazing paper, but you really didn't stick to the prompt?" Mom said.

"Yes. But that doesn't mean you would tell me if I looked . . ."

Mom kissed me on the top of my head. "I would tell you if you looked anything other than beautiful for your first day of middle school."

"And you know I wouldn't let you go to school looking like an idiot." Maisy grabbed a handful of granola from the open bag on the table. "Now let's go before we're late."

I was too nervous to talk, so Maisy filled our walk with the kind of chatter you aren't expected to respond to, like when the dental hygienist is cleaning your teeth. I focused on putting one foot in front of the other until we reached the flagpole in front of the middle school entrance, the designated spot for popular seventh graders.

Mia was sitting on top of the concrete flagpole base wearing a red jean skirt with a fitted white tank. She had the confidence of someone who never second-guessed her outfit or herself. Meghan sat by Mia's feet, wearing a red-and-white gingham sundress, with Madeline next to her in a white sundress dress with a thick red headband. Madison sat on the brick walkway wearing a white V-neck tee with a red skater skirt. Chloe, practically in her lap, wore the exact opposite—a red V-neck tee and a white skater skirt.

The seventh-grade boys were tossing a football on the lawn, but I could see a few of them taking peeks at the girls on the flagpole. The girls walking by couldn't help looking at the Royal Court to see what everyone would be wearing for the school year.

Maisy walked on the brick path to popularity like it was nothing. If you didn't count Maisy's brief stint at adventure camp, fitting in comes easy to her. In fact, the pact happened because she couldn't handle being an outsider, even if it was for only six weeks. Meanwhile, I couldn't help feeling like I had no business wearing Poppy Red, let alone walking anywhere near the path to popularity.

"Love your dress, Meghan," Maisy said.

Meghan rolled her eyes. "My mom made me wear it. I told her it was too extra, but she didn't listen."

"I just saw a post saying that gingham's the perfect transition print between summer and fall," I said, with one foot on the brick path and one foot off.

"Are you sure that wasn't a recycled post from two years ago?" Meghan asked.

"It was definitely new. Just can't remember if I saw it on Snapchat or Instagram." I realized that because of my lies, Meghan was never going to update her phone *and* she would be two seasons behind on fashion.

Meghan smiled at me. "Thanks."

Mia hopped off her perch. "First-day selfie?"

The girls pulled out their phones and used the cameras as mirrors while they reapplied lip gloss and smoothed down stray hairs. In sync, they all put their phones back in their pockets and squeezed together around the flagpole. They reminded me of a flock of birds who moved together as one.

I may have been wearing the signature M & M color, but that didn't mean I had earned a spot in their annual first-day-of-school Instagram post. Their photo from last year had spoken volumes to me about how I didn't have a place in Maisy's life anymore.

"Hurry up," Meghan said. "Before the bell rings."

"Come on, Bea," Maisy said.

I waited for someone to tell me I didn't belong in the picture. But Maisy tugged on my arm and suddenly I was huddled with the M & Ms. As we posed for selfie after selfie, it hit me that I wasn't going to be invisible this year.

"Think we got it," Mia finally said.

The girls broke their poses and crowded around her phone.

"Delete that one right now," Madison said. "I look cross-eyed."

"Ew. Delete that one too," Meghan said. "I look like a chipmunk."

All the pictures looked the same to me, but Madeline grabbed the phone. "We just need the right filter. I'll figure it out."

Then Meghan hissed, "He's coming."

"He looks even cuter today," Madison purred in a dreamy voice. "How is that even possible?"

"He has this whole undercover nerd thing going on," Maisy said. "Especially with those loafers."

"We need everyone to see us talking to him," Mia said. "Before Simone's friend group makes a move on him."

"Bea, get him over here," Madeline said, with a not-so-gentle shove in my back.

"Clark! Clark! Over here," I yelled across the grass.

"Did you have to be so obvious?" Madison said.

"Seriously," Chloe said.

"What's the purpose of getting him over here if no one sees?" Maisy said.

Maisy may not have the highest GPA, but her social IQ will always be higher than mine.

As Clark headed across the grass, every single girl, and a couple of guys, stared. Clark's status as Mapleton Middle School's Glow Up of the Year was official.

All the pact scheming over the summer had made me better at thinking on my feet. "Um, I can't remember when Robotics Club starts," I said, as soon as Clark got close enough.

He pushed his hair off his face. "Tomorrow during E block."

I smacked my head, like people do when they forget something important, but I did it so hard, it was highly probable I gave myself a concussion.

"Are you okay?" Clark asked.

I waved my hand. "Oh yeah, I do that all the time. I read this study that says it's a great way to wake your brain up."

Madison smacked herself in the side of the head. "Oooooh. I think it's working."

Clark adjusted his backpack. "You have to be really careful about what you read online. See you guys later."

Maisy shot me a look. If we really wanted to stake a claim on Clark, we needed him to stick with us at least until the bell rang. If I blew it with Clark on day one, I could kiss my Poppy Red days goodbye.

"Wait." I put my hand on his surprisingly hairy forearm, then dropped it almost immediately. "I've been thinking about the robotics competition. We should partner up."

Clark smiled broadly. "Griffin and Marshall will be psyched. We've got big plans this year, so we really need a fourth."

Last year Griffin Daley and Marshall Cooper went to Comic-Con dressed as Fortnite characters and weren't even embarrassed to post the pictures.

"Sounds great," I forced out.

The bell rang.

Clark took a step toward the school. "See you at the meeting."

Maisy shot me a look.

I walked a little closer to Clark. "What're you guys thinking about for this year?"

Clark was so excited to bounce robotics ideas off me that he didn't even notice he was surrounded by a sea of Poppy Red as we walked into school.

MAISY

"Ugh, my brain seriously hurts," I said, as Mia and I left math. "When are we ever going to use word problems in real life?"

"Never. We have Siri." Mia pulled a brush through her thick blond hair without dropping her math book.

As we turned the corner, I saw Bea standing in front of my locker.

"Mia, I'll meet you in the cafeteria," I said. "I have to drop some stuff off first."

"I'll wait." Mia shoved her brush in her pocketbook and flipped her hair over her shoulders.

"They might run out of smoothie bowls," I said. "I heard Mrs. Acres made her special granola topping."

Mia said, "See you in there." Then she headed down the hall, shooting off texts as she walked.

"I can't believe you're not in any of my classes," Bea said as soon as I got to my locker.

"That's because I don't want to fail middle school," I said. "Listen, I need to tell you something."

Bea's face crumpled up. "Oh no. The girls don't want me to sit with them at lunch?"

"No, it's not about that. But listen . . ." I started.

"Can't you just tell me on the walk to the caf—" Bea froze.

Mr. Pembrook was walking down the hall and straight toward us.

"That's what I was trying to tell you," I whispered.

Mr. Pembrook stopped in front of us and cleared his throat. He was wearing a bowtie that was covered in yellow pencils, pink erasers, and shiny red apples. Matching socks peeked out of the bottom of his too-short pants.

"Hi, Bea. Nice to see you again, Maisy," Mr. Pembrook said.

Bea narrowed her eyes at us. "Again?"

Mr. Pembrook straightened out his bowtie in a manic kind of way. "I, uh . . . got transferred to the middle school."

Bea's voice got higher with each syllable. "But I thought you only taught fifth grade?"

"I did up until this morning. Then, right in the middle of our staff meeting, Mr. Haim found out he made it on that reality show, you know the one where women compete to get engaged to one guy?" Mr. Pembrook said.

"OMG!" I shouted. "Mr. Haim is the new Bachelor? Why didn't you tell us in class?"

"You're Maisy's teacher?" Bea asked at the same time. "What about the honors section? Are you teaching that, too?"

"No, no, no." Now that Mr. Pembrook's bowtie was as straight as possible, he moved on to smoothing his beard. "Dr. Butterfield is teaching honors."

I got the feeling from his weird tone that he had to tell the principal he was dating Bea's mom and it turned into a whole thing.

Bea looked toward the cafeteria. "We have to go to lunch."

"Yeah, before the acai bowls sell out," I added, so Mr. Pembrook wouldn't feel bad.

"See you later," Mr. Pembrook said.

Bea's whole face tightened. "Later, as in literally or figuratively?"

"Um, for dinner . . . tonight . . . six p.m. Your mom's cooking," Mr. Pembrook said.

Before Bea could answer, Dr. Butterfield came out of nowhere and shoved an iPad under Mr. Pembrook's nose. "I tweaked Mr. Haim's lesson to fit the honors class, but now I'm not sure it meets the core curriculum standards. Can you take a quick look?"

Before Mr. Pembrook could answer, Bea grabbed my arm and dragged me down the hall.

"It's not that bad, Bea," I said, practically running to keep up with her.

"Did you see his bowtie? When people find out my mom's dating him . . ."

"People like Mr. Pembrook. He explains things so we can actually understand them," I said. "He even made up a rap song about the order of operations. It sounds cheesy, but I swear it wasn't."

Bea turned to me. "Would you want your mom dating him?"

Last night when I was trying to sleep, I couldn't stop picturing Mom sitting on her bed at rehab, staring at her phone, waiting for me to text back. I almost did. But then she would think that I had forgiven her and that what she did wasn't that bad. And maybe she would slip up. And maybe something really bad would happen this time. Addy can think I'm a jerk all she wants, but she doesn't realize I'm just trying to protect us.

Bea stopped walking. "I'm sorry. I didn't mean—"

I held up my hand. "It's fine."

"Seriously, I—" Bea started.

"Whatever you do, don't pull out your lunch bag. No one brings lunch," I said.

Bea's face crumpled. "But I didn't bring money."

"You can use my account. I have money left over from last year," I said.

"Thanks," Bea said.

I walked up to the food counter. "We'll have two smoothie bowls with your famous granola."

Mrs. Acres smiled at us. She had been our cafeteria lady since we were in kindergarten because our school district is so small that the elementary, middle, and high schools all share a cafeteria. "It's your lucky day. You girls got the last two."

Mrs. Acres topped our trays with acai bowls, and I paid with my account after grabbing us each a bottle of water.

Bea stood frozen at the entrance to the lunchroom holding her tray in front of her with shaky hands. "What if this is all a big mistake, Maisy? What if I say or do the wrong thing? Or even worse, what if I walk over to the table and they laugh at me when I try to sit down?"

"Didn't you hear Mrs. Acres?" I asked. "It's our lucky day."

CHAPTER EIGHT

BEA

THE PTA THOUGHT IT WOULD BE CUTE TO GIVE THE CAFETERIA A
"picnic theme," so they painted the walls with grassy meadows and
woodland creatures and replaced the long cafeteria tables with
picnic tables and benches. The M & Ms were sitting at the middle picnic table in the middle row, so they were literally the center
of everything.

Mia, Madeline, and Meghan sat on one bench, and Madison and
Chloe sat across from them on the other one. There was just enough
room for one more person at the popular table.

My hands wouldn't stop shaking and my water bottle rolled on
its side into my smoothie bowl. It took all of my strength not to drop
the tray. I realized I would have to back out of the cafeteria in front
of the whole school.

But Maisy walked over to Chloe like it was no big deal and said, "Scoot over so Bea and I can fit."

Madison and Chloe moved over, and Maisy plunked her tray down next to theirs. I settled on a tiny sliver of bench with half a butt cheek hanging over the edge. Sitting half on and half off the bench was a metaphor for my precarious status with the M & Ms.

Not only was my butt cheek hanging off, so was my tray. Maisy put my acai bowl and water on the end of the table and grabbed my tray and stacked it under hers. Such a simple solution, yet one I was not capable of figuring out in my anxious state.

Madeline scooped up a big spoonful of dark purple smoothie and granola. "Did you see Taylor Horvath?"

"Do you think she's going goth?" Madison asked.

"No, Madison." Mia rolled her eyes. "She's trying to be preppy with her black hair, black nail polish, and all-black clothes."

Madeline laughed and pointed her spoon at Madison. "Madison's always been the queen of obvious."

"Remember that time she asked Mrs. Palmer if she was having a baby *after* Mrs. Palmer told the class she was going on maternity leave?" Meghan teased.

"We were only in second grade back then." Madison's cheeks reddened as she stabbed at her acai bowl. "I didn't know what that meant."

"You mean her bowling-ball belly didn't clue you in?" Meghan joked.

Everyone laughed, but I noticed Madison's and Chloe's laughter was more forced.

I watched as the other girls skimmed the top of their smoothie bowls with their plastic spoons, capturing a thin layer of smoothie and granola before popping it in their mouths. I mimicked their action, before realizing that I don't like smoothie bowls. But now was not the time to be picky about food. I was willing to eat a whole plate of brussels sprouts if it meant not eating alone in the library.

Mia leaned in close. "Did you guys see Sutter walking to school alone? I heard her friend group dropped her."

"I heard it was because . . ." Madeline stabbed her plastic spoon in the air for emphasis, "they couldn't stand her B.O."

It took a lot of brain power to study the subtle nuances in their language and to figure out their speech patterns. But I was getting the hang of it.

I took a big swig of water. "Did you guys see Samantha's hair? Someone should leave a can of dry shampoo in her locker."

Madison and Chloe practically shrieked with laughter.

"OMG! That would be the best prank ever!" Meghan said.

Maisy shot a me a look.

"So, Genius Whisperer. What's the deal with Clark?" Madeline held up her phone. It showed a Snapchat picture of Clark standing with Simone, Mia's rival and the head of the second most popular friend group.

Mia cut in. "Simone's in his homeroom and she already put a picture with him on her story. Now everyone's gonna think he's with her friend group."

"Oh, heck no," Meghan said.

"What's your plan, Bea?" Mia asked.

"Yeah, what's your plan?" Madison echoed.

My heart sank as I realized having one plan wasn't going to be enough to make it with these girls. I was going to have to come up with new plans all the time, which was Maisy's strength, not mine.

MAISY

Last year it didn't bother me when the M & Ms spent the lunch period trash-talking the other girls in the grade. Talking about how Emily Robbins got her period while wearing white jeans in the middle of English class or how Tisha Stevens had a huge crush on Peter Hutchins when he was obviously in love with her best friend helped distract me from the Mom situation. But after spending the summer with the Sunflower girls, I realized there are so many more interesting things to talk about than other people.

Part of me wanted to mess this up for Bea, mess this up for us, so we could go sit somewhere else, just the two of us. Eating lunch in the library with Bea sounded pretty good to me. At least then we could both be ourselves, like at camp.

But Bea looked at me with her big brown eyes, begging me to fix this for her.

"Bea was just telling me her idea when we were buying lunch," I said.

"What's the plan, Bea?" Madeline asked, while she scraped the sides of her plastic bowl for every last bit of purple acai goodness.

Two red dots appeared on Bea's cheeks, and her freckles flashed through her thick layer of concealer. "Um, Maisy can explain it better."

"Bea's partnering up with Clark, Griffin, and Marshall for the robotics competition. It's the perfect way to hang out with him as much as possible," I said.

Mia rolled her eyes. "We *already* knew that."

"That isn't really a plan," Meghan said.

"And it doesn't have anything to do with us," Madeline added.

"That's only the first part." I grabbed a big cluster of granola off Bea's bowl and popped it in my mouth. "Last year they won with a drone that takes selfies and posts to social media."

"My mom showed me a video of it on the school website," Madeline said. "It's actually really cool. You don't have to worry about someone holding the phone to take the picture, and everyone fits in the shot."

"Holding the phone is the worst," Meghan said. "Whoever holds the phone always has a gigantic head compared to the other people."

"Agreed!" Mia said.

"And it posts right to Instagram," Madeline said.

"I bet they could, like, sell it for real," Madison said.

"I would totally buy one," Chloe chimed in.

"What does their drone have to do with us?" Mia asked.

Bea jumped in. "We get Clark to your house by telling him we want to experiment with the drone in a social setting. Then we post pics with him so everyone knows we landed the Glow Up of the Year," Bea said.

Mia held up two fingers. "There are two problems with this plan."

Bea's face crumpled and I could feel her body tense up next to me. "What?"

"You mean who," Madeline said.

Mia waved her arms around. "Have you seen Marshall and Griffin lately?"

"OMG!" Madison shrieked. "Did you see what Marshall's wearing?"

Before anyone could answer, Madison blurted out, "A Minecraft shirt!"

I leaned into the table and lowered my voice. "What seventh-grade boy is going to hang out with a bunch of girls by himself? Especially girls as popular as us."

Mia sighed. "Good point."

"Who said anything about Marshall and Griffin being in the pictures? We can crop those two losers out of the photos," Bea said.

Bea was morphing into an M & M faster than I thought she would.

Mia looked at Bea with respect. "Good plan."

Madison and Chloe both nodded and said, "Good plan."

Mia plopped a bright yellow plastic bag from Forever 21 on the table. The bag crinkled as she reached inside and pulled out a Poppy Red scrunchie. She scraped her blond hair into a high ponytail and wrapped the scrunchie around it.

"OMG! So cute!" Madison said.

"Yeah, so cute," Chloe chimed in.

Mia reached in the bag slowly and pulled out another scrunchie. She handed it to Meghan. "We need to keep our brand on point."

"Love it!" Meghan bunched her wavy hair into a messy bun and wrapped the scrunchie around it. "This way everyone will know who's in our group."

I could feel Bea's body freeze while Mia reached in the bag and handed Madeline and Madison scrunchies. Madeline put her scrunchie on her wrist and Madison pulled her limp hair into a low ponytail.

I wasn't giving in to Mia's little waiting game. I reached in the bag and pulled out a scrunchie. "Thanks," I said, twisting my hair into a loose braid.

Mia stared at me while I wrapped the end of the braid with the Poppy Red fabric. Then she folded her arms across her chest. "Sorry, Chloe and Bea. There aren't enough for everyone. I only got enough for the original M & Ms."

"That's okay," Chloe said, in a breathless rush, with an expression on her face that made it clear she was definitely not okay.

Bea blinked and said in a small voice, "It's fine."

"Very funny, Mia," I said. "I felt more scrunchies in there."

"JK!!!" Mia laughed. "You should've seen your faces." She reached in the bag and pulled out the last scrunchies.

She handed one to Chloe, who smiled like she had just been given a hundred-dollar bill.

Chloe held it in her hand for a full minute before pulling it over her wrist. "Thank you, Mia. I'll wear it every day."

Mia held out her hand in front of Bea's face with the last scrunchie in it. Bea reached for it, but Mia snapped her hand into a fist. "Just make sure your plan works."

"It'll work," Bea said. "I swear."

Mia opened her hand. Bea grabbed the scrunchie and pulled her straight red hair up into a copycat version of Mia's high ponytail.

⇥·· CHAPTER NINE ··⇤

BEA

"I WAS SO NERVOUS WHEN WE WALKED ACROSS THE CAFETERIA," I practically shouted over the food processor.

"Why? You were already in the M & Ms' back-to-school photo on Instagram." Mom turned off the machine and squirted fresh lemon juice into the green sludge. "I saw it when I got to work. I was relieved because you looked so happy."

"You know when you dream of something happening? Then it finally does and you're waiting for someone to tell you it's all a big mistake?" I asked.

Mom poured the green mixture into a glass dressing decanter and gave it a hearty shake. "Don't laugh, but that's how I felt about Gavin. It's not like I dreamed of dating a vegan math teacher with a bowtie collection that rivals my shoe closet."

I tried to adjust my facial expression so Mom couldn't see my dismay at the direction our conversation had taken.

"But I really hoped I would find someone who gets me." Mom looked up at the ceiling. "Someone who appreciates my weirdness. Someone who would make me believe in love again. Once I found that, I was convinced it was a big mistake. I was certain Gavin would text me to say he had been temporarily insane thinking we would work."

"When did you stop worrying?" I asked.

"When we both got food poisoning from that all-you-can-eat burrito place," Mom said. "You know the one at Maple Grove Shopping Center?"

I grimaced. "Talk about a questionable place for a date."

"We realized that about an hour after dinner. But when you go through a weekend chugging Imodium and taking turns using the only bathroom and you're still cracking jokes and enjoying each other, you know it's for real," Mom said.

"Let's hope I don't have to get diarrhea with the M & Ms to know it's for real," I said.

Mom put one hand on each side of my face. "Just make sure you aren't so wrapped up in the dream of being popular that you don't really get to know these girls. You need to figure out if they're people you actually want to be friends with."

"Okay, Mom," I said. "No one brings lunch in middle school. We all get acai bowls."

"Everyone thinks acai bowls are healthy, but they're packed with sugar. You may as well eat a bowl of ice cream for lunch," Mom said.

"I won't get one every day. I swear. But no one brings lunch in middle school," I said.

Mom pulled a twenty out of the pocket of her linen overalls. "Make sure you buy real food with this."

"Thanks." I shoved the money in my cell phone case. "Speaking of real food, what do we feed a vegan for dinner?"

"Sweet potato and black bean burgers, with green goddess salad on the side," said Mom. "Don't worry, it's going to be delicious."

"Does this mean we have to turn vegan now?" I asked.

"Let's make a deal. I won't make you turn vegan if you don't turn me into a carnivore," said a deep voice from behind me.

I spun around so fast the ends of my hair whipped my face. Mr. Pembrook was standing in my kitchen. He had swapped out the button-down shirt and bowtie for a red Gryffindor T-shirt and black joggers. It was weird enough to see a teacher in street clothes; having him standing in my kitchen made my brain feel like it would explode.

Mr. Pembrook reached out his closed fist with a lame smile on his face. Mom looked at me expectantly, so I gave him a fist bump back. Why does every grown-up in the world think they look cool when they give a fist bump?

Mom ran over to Mr. Pembrook and looked like she was about to hug him, but then she took a step back with her hands dangling awkwardly at her sides. "I made a copycat recipe of the sweet potato burger you love from Vegan Underground. I even made the green goddess salad with the shaved turnips. With chocolate chia pudding for dessert."

Mr. Pembrook rubbed his nonexistent belly. "Sounds like the best first-day-of-school meal."

I shuddered. "Maybe for you."

"You're going to love it, Bea." Mom pulled a stack of plates from the cabinet. "And if you don't, there's always PB and J."

I know lots of moms give the "There's always PB and J speech," but I had never heard it because it had been just Mom and me for so long, and we both like all the same exact things.

Until Mr. Pembrook came along.

Mr. Pembrook took drinking glasses out of the cabinet like he owned the place. "Did Bea tell you the news?"

"That she sat at the popular table at lunch?" Mom said.

I shot Mom daggers from my eyes, but she was so busy pouring Mr. Pembrook a tall glass of oat milk, she didn't even notice.

"This is going to be anticlimactic compared to Bea's news." Mr. Pembrook grabbed a set of salad tongs from what Mom calls our miscellaneous drawer and scooped up salad onto our plates. "I got transferred to the middle school."

Mom popped open a pack of gluten-free burger buns because, apparently, you can't go vegan without riding the gluten-free train as well. "You've been dying to teach middle school! But how did this happen so last minute? I hope Dr. Butterfield's okay. He wasn't looking so good at the middle school orientation."

Mr. Pembrook laughed. "Dr. Butterfield's fine. He would be a lot better if he cut back on all the butter though." He winked at Mom and me. Mom laughed like it was the funniest thing she had ever heard.

I grabbed a handful of silverware and started setting the table. "Mr. Haim's going to be the next Bachelor."

"Does this mean we have to give up our feminist boycott and actually watch this season?" Mom asked.

Mr. Pembrook brought our plates to the table, all three at once, like a waiter. "I offered to take over his classes if Butterfield covered the honors classes, because, well ... you know." His eyes darted no-so-subtly toward me.

"Oh, Gavin," Mom said, with a sad smile. "I know how much you want to teach honors."

Mr. Pembrook smiled. "I'm sure Bea doesn't want her mom's boyfriend teaching her math."

I also didn't want my old math teacher calling himself my mom's boyfriend or eating dinner at my house, but that hadn't stopped him.

I sat down in my usual spot next to Mom, but then Mr. Pembrook sat down and I ended up in the middle. Anyone looking in the window would think we were a family.

Mom wrinkled her brow. "Can you get in trouble if Mr. Sellers finds out about . . ." Mom waved her hands around the table. "This?"

"That you're the best vegan cook on this side of Mapleton?" Mr. Pembrook asked through a mouthful of bean burger.

Mom laughed like he was a comedian. "Gavin, you know what I mean."

He smiled. "I told Mr. Sellers about us."

I tried not to gag on my salad greens.

Mr. Pembrook speared a forkful of lettuce. "Mr. Sellers said it was fine as long as I didn't teach any of Bea's classes."

I took a big bite of burger, which tasted like refried beans mashed with sweet potatoes, definitely not foods that are meant to be together. I had never been more relieved in my life to have my phone ring.

Mom shook her head at me. "Bea, no phone at the table."

"But it's Dad. He's probably calling to see how the first day of school went," I said.

"Okay, but be quick so your burger doesn't get cold," Mom said.

"Does it matter if a veggie burger gets cold?" I asked, then scraped my chair back.

Mr. Pembrook laughed. "Not really."

Mom waved her hand at me. "Go ahead."

I walked into the living room with my phone held up to my ear. "Hey, Dad."

As soon as I sank into the couch, Mr. Pebbles leapt onto my lap and tucked himself in for a snuggle session.

"Hi, Bea! It's Monica," my future stepmom's Splenda-sweet voice said.

I rolled my eyes at Mr. Pebbles. "Loved the proposal video."

"Thank you," Monica gushed. "Jimmy's so good at surprises."

I thought about how I was the last person to find out he was getting married. But I kept my voice even. "Oh, yeah. He's the master of surprises."

"Are you free next Saturday?" Monica asked.

"Yes," I said, eager to finally see the new house, hoping my basement room wasn't as depressing as it looked on FaceTime.

"Great!" Monica said. "We're having a girls' day. Peyton, Vivi, you, and me."

"What about Dad?" I scanned my mental calendar and realized I hadn't seen Dad since a couple of weeks before I left for camp.

Monica giggled. "Jimmy can't come dress shopping with us! It's bad luck for the groom to see the wedding dress before the big day."

"We're going dress shopping?"

"We're going to have the best day ever! We're picking out bridesmaid dresses. Then we can do a special lunch," Monica said.

"The girls really want to get to know you better."

For girls who were so eager to get to know me, I could count on one hand the combined number of words they had said to me the few times I had seen them.

Monica filled the silence. "I want you to be involved every step of the way. And we need to hustle because the wedding's right around the corner."

I forced out a happy tone. "Can't wait! I have to go, though. It's dinnertime."

"I'll pick you up next Saturday at nine," Monica said. "Enjoy your dinner."

Sometimes, I think it would be easier to have a mean stepmother—someone who didn't want me in their life. But the sad thing was, Monica tried harder than Dad.

I was about to stand up, but then I heard Mom and Mr. Pembrook laughing. I snuggled Mr. Pebbles tighter to avoid going back into the kitchen where my imitation burger on a fake bun and another potential stepparent were waiting for me.

MAISY

A few hours after I got home from school, my house was actually quiet for the first time since camp. Dad had two hip replacements on his surgery schedule, which meant he probably wouldn't be home till midnight, and Grandma was at the gym watching Addy's practice. I don't know who was more obsessed with Addy qualifying for level ten, Addy or Grandma.

Grandma left me a frozen dinner of fried chicken, corn, and mashed potatoes. The picture on the box made the food look as good as KFC, but when I took the microwavable container out, the food was shriveled up and rock hard. At least when I was in charge of things, I made actual food for us.

I had already showered, laid out my clothes for the morning, and finished my homework. So I tucked myself into my loft bed with my laptop, my favorite cozy blanket, and a whole summer's worth of Netflix to catch up on. But I couldn't stop thinking about Mom. Lately, whenever I tried to relax, she popped up in my thoughts.

When she first went away, I Googled her rehab place. It supposedly had one of the highest success rates for its patients. But I couldn't help wondering—what if Mom was in worse shape than the other people? What if she was going to be the person who brought their percentage down? What if she came home and tricked us into thinking she was better, and she really wasn't? She had gotten really good at lying over the past couple of years.

My laptop pinged with a FaceTime request from Bea. I accepted it and my screen lit up with Bea's face. She looked more like the old Bea from camp, in her beat-up Camp Amelia T-shirt and her freckles spattered all over her makeup-free face. But she had that stressed-out look that had been on her face since we got off the bus in Mapleton.

"What's the matter?" I asked.

Bea leaned into the screen so close that I could see up her nostrils. "Peyton and Vivi are following me on Instagram."

"Those little jerks!" I scrunched up my face. "What were they thinking?"

Bea laughed. "I'm being crazy, aren't I?"

"They are going to be related to you in a few months. I could see why they would follow you," I said. "They're probably trying to get to know you better."

"That's the problem!" Bea cried. "Now they're going to know what a nerd I am. I posted three times last year and two of the posts were of Mr. Pebbles and the other one is from when Mom and I went to the . . . wait for it . . . Renaissance Fair."

"I saw that post with your mom. It was cute," I said.

"I was holding a giant turkey leg!" Bea shouted. "And Mom and I were dressed up in medieval dresses. Now they know I'm a total weirdo and a social reject."

"You've never had sisters before. I could care less how popular Addy is. All I worry about is her stealing my clothes and having my back with Dad. We also have an agreement that she watches *Pitch Perfect* with me whenever I want, as long as I binge-watch old seasons of *Degrassi* with her," I said.

"It's different for you guys. You're actually related. You have all this shared history," Bea said.

I exhaled really hard. "Right now, it would be better if we didn't have shared history. She thinks I'm the worst person in the world for not forgiving Mom."

Bea smiled. "Addy never could stay mad for too long. You guys just have different personalities."

"My personality has a lot more common sense than hers," I said.

"At least you'll have each other when your mom comes home," Bea said.

"I guess," I said.

Bea held up her phone. "Look how many friends Peyton has! And she got four hundred and twenty-three likes on her last post. Four hundred and twenty-three!"

"You need to put your phone down," I said.

Bea groaned. "Just when things are on track with the M & Ms, there's another group of pretty girls who won't want to include me."

My door swung open and Dad walked in with a big smile on his face.

"Gotta go," I said. "My dad's home. Seriously, put your phone away." I snapped my laptop shut.

"Looks like someone's enjoying her new room," Dad said.

"That's 'cause Addy's not here. What're you doing home so early?"

"My last surgery got canceled because the patient had a fever," Dad said.

I threw off my blankets and climbed down from my bed.

"Grandma told me she left you dinner," he said.

I groaned, picturing the TV dinner waiting for me in the microwave. "Please don't make me eat it. It reminds me of the freeze-dried food they made us eat when that astronaut came to visit on career day."

"Grandma's working hard to take care of us. Come eat your dinner," Dad said.

I followed him down the stairs and into the kitchen as slowly as possible.

"What's all this?" I asked, as soon as I walked in the kitchen, waving my arms at the counters that were covered in grocery shopping bags.

Dad pulled on his King of the Grill apron. "Did you really think I was going to make you eat a TV dinner? My brother and I ate so many of those things growing up; I still gag whenever I see the cardboard box."

"Thank God!" I said.

Dad rolled up his sleeves. "Wash your hands so you can help. You're on salad duty."

He pulled out a couple of packs of chicken cutlets. "I'm going to make enough for a couple of days so all you guys have to do is reheat them."

"Thank you for saving me from Grandma's 'cooking.'"

I pulled out a bag of prewashed spring mix and smiled because Dad remembered it's the only kind of lettuce I like. I opened the bag and dumped the lettuce mix into a big wooden salad bowl.

Dad cracked eggs into a glass bowl. "How was the first day of school?"

I dumped the carton of cherry tomatoes into a colander and ran water over them. "Okay, I guess."

"Your first day of middle school was just okay?" Dad asked, beating the eggs. "Wasn't it nice to have Bea hanging out with you and the other Skittles?"

I threw a dish towel at him. "Dad! You know we're the M & Ms."

He dipped a piece of chicken in the eggs, then into a plate filled with breadcrumbs. "Were the girls nice to Bea?"

"Yeah," I said. "But since I came back from camp, I've been noticing all these things about the M & Ms that never bothered me before. Did you ever come back from being away and feel like you don't even remember why you liked certain people in the first place?"

"Not really. But it's different with guys. You play baseball, they play baseball, so you're friends. I didn't really think too much about it when I was a kid. Then in college and medical school, I was studying so much that I didn't have time for a social life. I have work friends now, of course, but your mom's really my best friend," Dad said. "She's the only one besides you girls I want to spend time with more than anything."

"Is she still?" I asked, keeping my eyes down on the cucumber I was slicing. "Your best friend?"

Dad dropped the chicken in a skillet and the hot oil hissed and popped. "Of course she is. You don't stop being best friends with someone just because they get sick." He looked right at me. "Maisy, nobody's perfect."

I didn't need my mom to be perfect. I just needed her to be her self again, but I was pretty certain she had forgotten how to be the old Mom.

→·· CHAPTER TEN ··←

BEA

A LIGHT BREEZE SWAYED THE TREE BRANCHES AS A REMINDER that fall was here, but it hadn't stopped the girls from swimming.

"Come in," Mia called from her perch on the unicorn float. She was wearing a simple black bathing suit that probably retailed for a hundred dollars. "My dad put the heater all the way up, so it feels like bathwater."

Mom always worries about the heat bill. We get through the winter months by keeping the thermostat at sixty-six and extra quilts on our beds. Everything about Mia's life was so easy compared to mine.

Maisy burrowed her arms deeper into her sweatshirt. "It's too cold."

"You'll warm up as soon as you get in," Madison called from the donut float where she was huddled with Chloe. Madison was wearing a black-and-white bikini top with neon yellow bottoms, and Chloe was wearing the neon yellow top with black-and-white bottoms.

Maisy jerked her head toward Madison and Chloe and whispered, "They're becoming the same person."

I pretended not to hear. I couldn't risk getting caught gossiping about the M & Ms, not even the low-ranking ones.

The gate squeaked open and Clark walked in looking like he came from a Hollister photo shoot. Griffin trailed behind him wearing black bathing suit bottoms; the outline of every single bone from his clavicle to his rib cage was on display. Marshall had a stripe of thick white sunblock on the bridge of his nose and across both cheeks. He was wearing a long-sleeved rash guard and board shorts that came almost to his ankles. The tiny bit of skin that poked out was covered in angry-looking eczema.

"Bea, you're supposed to be the smart one." Mia hopped off her unicorn float and glared at me. "I knew this was a bad idea."

I felt my cheeks burn and my legs turn weak.

"They just got here," hissed Maisy. "Give it a chance."

"If anyone finds out Griffin and Marshall swam in my pool, no one will ever come over again," Mia said.

I thought being invisible was the worst possible scenario, but having Mia Atwater look at me with revulsion was a new low.

Maisy walked over to the covered patio area where the guys were huddled around a big black suitcase. "What's in the suitcase?"

"Cue the music," Clark said.

Marshall unzipped the suitcase with a flourish and pulled out a Bluetooth speaker, and robotic techno filled the backyard.

Madeline and Meghan ran over to the guys. Mia stared at them for what seemed like an eternity, before she sighed and got out of the pool to investigate. Not surprisingly, Madison and Chloe were right at her heels.

Madeline squatted next to the black suitcase, trying to get a closer look, even though Marshall had zipped it back up. "Are you guys gonna do magic tricks for us?"

Madison squealed, "I love magic tricks!"

"Me too!" Chloe said.

Griffin wheeled the suitcase into the middle of Mia's grotto and spun it around.

Madison grabbed Marshall's arm. "Is there a rabbit in there?"

Clark shook his head and said, "No rabbit." He pulled out pairs of giant goggles and passed them to Griffin and Marshall.

When the music built to a crescendo, the guys ceremoniously pulled down their goggles onto their faces in unison.

Marshall sounded like someone was holding his nose closed. "Always remember, safety first."

The girls laughed, and not in a mean way either. Mia and Madeline leaned over to try to get a look inside the black suitcase, but

Griffin swatted them away. "You don't want to ruin the surprise," he said.

The music hit another crescendo as Clark pulled a gigantic aluminum canister from the suitcase and plunked it on the ground.

A chorus of oohs and aahs filled the yard.

Griffin pulled out a giant silver bowl, like the one Mom uses for chopped salads, and Marshall pulled out a bag of sugar, a carton of heavy cream, and a bottle of vanilla extract.

"Omg! I think they're making ice cream!" Madeline shouted.

"It's like that new place that just opened up at the mall," Mia said, with an air of authority.

"Nitro?" asked Maisy.

"Yeah, that's the one," Mia nodded, as if it had been her idea all along to bring Clark, Griffin, and Marshall over to make us nitrous ice cream.

I snapped the scrunchie, which felt safe on my wrist.

"Where did you guys get the nitrous?" Madeline asked.

Clark winked. "Chem Club gets keys to the lab."

"Nerd perks." Griffin grinned.

The girls giggled.

Griffin poured a mountain of sugar into the bowl. Marshall opened a container of cream and poured some on top. Then Griffin added a teaspoon of vanilla extract.

Clark pulled on thick industrial gloves, like the kind Mom wears when she cleans the gutters. He opened the nitrous container and smoke billowed out like we were in a haunted house.

Mia started narrating an Insta story. "We're making nitro ice cream here in my backyard!" She held her phone over the bowl while Clark stirred. "Look at that consistency! It's turning into ice cream!"

"Careful!" Maisy grabbed Mia's hand. "Your hand's gonna freeze off."

"Safety first," Griffin, Marshall, and Clark said in unison.

The girls laughed and Mia pulled her hand back.

"Can someone grab bowls?" Clark asked.

Madison and Chloe ran to the outdoor kitchen area and grabbed bowls and spoons.

Clark took an ice cream scoop from the suitcase and filled a bowl with ice cream. He had clearly figured out how things worked with the M & Ms because he handed the first bowl to Mia.

Mia passed her phone to Meghan so Meghan could film her. She didn't even worry about getting Griffin and Marshall in the shot.

Mia took the first spoonful and blew smoke from her nose and mouth like a dragon while Meghan captured every second.

The girls shrieked with delight, shouting things like, "Let me try!" and "Watch this!" while Mia posted on Instagram.

MAISY

If the boys had to wear gloves to protect their hands from the nitrous, how could it be safe to put it in food? What if I breathed it in and my lungs froze? Everyone was so busy posting videos on Instagram and Snapchat, no one noticed I was munching away on Doritos instead.

"Hilary Mishkoff commented on my post!" Mia shouted.

Madeline grabbed Mia's phone. "Let me see!"

Meghan leaned over Madeline's shoulder. "OMG! What did she say?"

Clark turned to me. "Who's Hilary Mishkoff?"

"The most popular girl in tenth grade. See. She has three thousand followers."

Clark's jaw dropped. "Seriously?"

I nodded. "She's a legend. *Everyone* follows her."

"I don't. At least I don't think I do. Sometimes my sister messes with my Instagram. Let me check." Clark picked up his phone, and his eyes grew wide when he saw all his Instagram follower notifications. "What the heck?"

I leaned over his shoulder. "Looks like you might be catching up to Hilary Mishkoff."

Clark scrolled his finger down his phone screen. He wrinkled his forehead. "Why would all these people follow me?"

"Because I tagged you in my post," Mia said.

Clark stared at his phone. "But they don't even know me."

"They wanna know you now," Meghan said, while she ran her finger along her bowl for the last licks of ice cream.

"You want even more followers?" Madeline jumped up. "Let's post a drone pic!"

Clark shrugged. "Seems like I already have enough followers."

"From the pool," Mia said, as if she didn't even hear Clark. "Everyone get on the floats."

We headed to the pool. Marshall and Griffin didn't think twice before jumping in the pool and climbing on the firecracker popsicle float. Luckily, the girls loved their ice cream so much they forgot all about their plan to leave Marshall and Griffin out of social media posts.

I grabbed the hamburger float from the side of Mia's pool house and brought it to the edge of the pool so that I could climb on it without getting wet. Bea held on to the float while I climbed on, then she came aboard.

"Chloe and Madison, there's room for you guys, too," Bea said.

I scooted over and waved them to our float. Chloe flashed me a grateful smile and I felt like a jerk for being so judgy about her.

Mia pouted her lips and said in a babyish tone, "I'm all alone. Clark come sit with me."

Clark flipped off the diving board into the water and Mia laughed when he splashed water everywhere. He climbed on her donut float and Mia scooted in as close to him as possible, but Clark was so focused on getting his drone ready to take a selfie that he didn't notice.

"Hey, Reg! Wake up," Clark said.

The drone, which had been sitting on one of the tables, unnoticed by all of us, lit up and flew above Clark's head.

"Hey, Reg! Selfie mode," Clark said.

The drone made a whirring sound as it flew to the pool area, then hovered lower so it was the perfect height to take a selfie from above.

"How does the drone know where to take the picture?" Madeline asked.

"Heat sensors," Griffin said.

"Hey, Reg! A little to the left," Clark said.

The M & Ms all got into their perfect picture poses, lips slightly pouted, toes pointed, eyes wide, as the drone lit up with each selfie.

Suddenly, everyone was crowded around Marshall, arguing about which picture was the best. Of course, Marshall had also invented an app that fixes pretty much any picture blunder, so the girls were shouting orders at him like, "Fix my wonky eye!" and "Can you cover my pimple?" and "Can you smooth out my hair?"

Clark stacked up the ice cream bowls and brought them to the sink. So I followed with all of the spoons and empty water bottles.

"You named your drone Reg?" I asked.

"Reginald Denny invented the first large-scale drone back in the thirties," Clark said. "It was much bigger than this one, but it was the first aircraft of its kind."

I laughed. "You might be the first person I've ever met who's smarter than Bea."

"Not true," said Clark. "Bea usually beats me in math."

"I bet not by much," I said.

Clark dumped the dishes in the sink. "Bea thinks we should do a Reg 2.0 for the fair this year. But I don't know what else he could do."

"Since Reg can already figure out how to fly above people, maybe he can squirt out sunblock, too? No one ever wants to get out of the pool to get the sunblock. Skin cancer is a serious thing, you know. Just think of how many lazy people you could be saving."

Clark tilted his head to the side and squinted.

I whipped my hair up into a quick topknot. "Please forget I said that. I say dumb things sometimes."

"Are you kidding?" Clark said. "It's a great idea, and I think it might actually work. We just need to build a chamber to hold the sunblock and create the dispenser."

Feeling a burst of confidence, I said, "Also, since Reg is hooked up to social media anyway, maybe you can hook him up to Apple Music or Spotify so he can play music too?"

Clark stared at me.

"What? Do I have something on my face?" I rubbed the sides of my mouth and my chin.

"No. I was just thinking that I totally get why Bea is friends with you. You are way smarter than you let on," Clark said.

→·· CHAPTER ELEVEN ··←

BEA

MOM BROUGHT OUR BREAKFAST DISHES TO THE SINK AND RAN HOT water over them. "You're going to be late."

"I'm waiting for Maisy."

Mom looked at her watch. "Maybe she slept through her alarm. Or she's sick. I heard strep is going around. But you need to leave, with or without her."

The apple cinnamon oatmeal I had just scarfed down was sitting like lead in the pit of my stomach. "I need Maisy. These girls aren't my real friends yet."

Mom raised an eyebrow. "Is this how you made friends at camp? By being scared and hiding behind someone else?"

"I was in first grade when I went to camp for the first time. I didn't know enough to be nervous."

"Exactly. Walk up to that flagpole like you belong, and the girls will treat you like you do," Mom said.

"You make it sound so easy," I said.

"You make it sound so hard," Mom said. "Maybe it's somewhere in the middle."

The knot in my stomach got tighter as I thought about walking up to the flagpole alone. "I hope you're right."

"I'm always right." Mom grabbed her purse from the kitchen counter. "I'll drop you off."

Mom pulled up to the school, and we spotted the M & Ms standing around the flagpole. Compared to the sea of multicolored outfits circulating on the school lawn, the M & Ms stood out in Poppy Red, making them look like the popularity powerhouses they were.

Mom parked at the curb. I looked at the dashboard clock. Six minutes till the first bell. Six minutes that would seem like an eternity if the M & Ms ignored me.

I breathed out hard and reached for the door handle.

"Wait." Mom grabbed my arm. "You need to think about how you feel at camp. Think about how confident you are when you step on those camp grounds."

"There's no way I could even come close to feeling like that now," I said.

Mom looked me right in the eyes. "Then fake it. No one will know the difference."

My mom, who doesn't believe in dyeing the wiry gray hairs sprouting in her wild curls, was advocating faking it. This only made me realize how desperate my situation was.

I walked toward the flagpole, wondering if I was ever going to really feel like I fit in.

Madison ran up to me. "Where did you get that lip gloss?"

"Yeah, where's it from?" Chloe asked.

"Bath and Body Works," I said.

"It's Poppy Red!" Mia said.

I pulled out the tube. "You guys can borrow some."

While Mia swiped on my lip gloss, I flicked my eyes over to Mom's car and gave a barely perceptible nod. Mom smiled at me, even though she always tells me not to share things like drinks and lip gloss. Then she drove off in the direction of her office.

"Where's Maisy?" Chloe asked.

My stomach lurched at the reminder that Maisy and I came as a package deal, much like Chloe and Madison. There was no way Chloe would dare step foot near the flagpole without Madison by her side, and I couldn't believe I had been so bold only two weeks into my new-found status as a probationary M & M.

I shrugged. "I think she's sick."

Mia held up her phone. "Our drone selfie has even more likes than my ice cream post."

"Wow," I said, temporary relief flooding through me. I looked at the clock that hung over the school entrance. Two minutes till the bell rang. A hundred and twenty seconds of saying and doing the right thing without Maisy.

"Did anyone get through that science packet?" Meghan asked.

Mia groaned. "Um, no. I swear Mrs. Finnegan is trying to torture us."

"When's it due?" I asked.

"Tomorrow," Meghan said. "But it's so hard, none of us are ever going to finish it."

"I told you guys I can help," Madeline said. "It's really not that bad."

"You are the worst at explaining," Mia said. "You yell at us when we don't understand what you're saying. And you won't just give us the answers."

"I'm not gonna risk breaking the honor code when we all have the same answers on our homework," Madeline said.

"I can help," I said. "You won't have to worry about me having the same answers because I'm not in your class."

"That would be awesome!" Mia said. "Let's all go to my house after school today."

Helping with homework? I could do that in my sleep. Relief flooded through me.

But then, out of the corner of my eye, I spotted Mr. Pembrook walking toward us holding a unicycle under one arm. Everyone knows he's obsessed with the environment, but couldn't he at least ride a bike to work like a normal person?

"You guys, Hollister is having a huge sale!" Madison said.

I leaned over her phone pretending to be absorbed with the sale items, even though Mom had a rule about not buying more clothes after our big back-to-school shopping trip.

Out of the corner of my eye, I could see Mr. Pembrook getting closer to us, and I prayed the ground would open up and swallow me whole. He was wearing a bowtie with tacos all over it. Matching taco socks peeked out from the three inches between the hem of his khaki pants and his brown loafers. If you Google Imaged "nerdy teacher," Mr. Pembrook would probably pop up first in the search.

As he got closer, I could see it happening in slow motion, him reaching out his fist ready to give me a fist bump. At school. In front of everyone.

I have to admit, it wasn't my proudest moment, but he didn't give me any other choice. The bell rang, and I turned my back and headed to class, pretending I didn't see him.

MAISY

As soon as I woke up, I knew something was going on. I could smell the warm bagels from Bagelville before I got to the kitchen. Dad gets home from work pretty late, so he doesn't usually wake up early enough for a bagel run, unless we have something to celebrate like a birthday or something to worry about like a big test.

Dad pulled out glasses from the cupboard and started filling them with fresh-squeezed orange juice. "Morning, girls."

Addy reached in the brown paper bag and pulled out a poppy seed bagel. "You got bagels!"

I grabbed a warm everything bagel and said, "That's what it looks like, genius."

Grandma shook her head at me, while she emptied a packet of Splenda into her coffee. "Be nice to your sister."

Dad handed us both tall glasses of orange juice and gave Grandma a look.

Grandma grabbed her mug and said, "I'm going to putter around in the garden."

Now I knew something was definitely up, because unless her friend Bernadette is FaceTiming her, Grandma is scared to do anything in the garden because she's worried about messing it up. Also, Grandma was still wearing her pajamas, and she never leaves the house unless she is fully dressed and her "face is on."

Addy was taking monster-sized bites of her bagel and barely chewing before she swallowed. She would be on bagel number two any minute. Meanwhile, I was still spreading vegetable cream cheese on mine, because I couldn't take a bite till I knew what was going on.

Dad said, "I got two dozen so we can freeze the rest. My residents will eat anything, so I'll bring the rest of the Lender's to work."

"You should bring them the TV dinners, too," I said.

"Good idea." Dad laughed for a minute, but then his face turned serious. "So, girls, I have news."

"What?" Addy said, through a mouthful of partially chewed bagel and gobs of cream cheese.

"Ew! No one wants to see what you're eating!" I said, handing her a napkin.

Dad took a long sip of coffee and gave us "the look," which meant to knock it off. "Sorry to start the morning with a big talk, but this is the only time of day I can guarantee we will all be home, and awake," Dad gave a nervous chuckle, "at the same time."

"What's going on?" Addy asked.

"Um, hello? Mom's obviously coming home," I blurted out.

It wasn't until the words came out of my mouth that the reality hit.

Addy looked at Dad. He silently nodded.

We sat in silence for less than a minute, which is all Addy needed to process the news and start talking about herself.

She jumped up so fast she spilled her glass of orange juice all over the table. "I can't wait to show Mom my level-nine routines. She's going to be shocked when she sees what I can do now. Is she coming to the first meet?"

I grabbed a roll of paper towels and started mopping up the mess no one else seemed worried about. "Wow! Self-centered much?"

Addy turned to me. "Why are you always so mean?"

"We just got this *huge* news and all you can talk about is gymnastics," I said. "All you ever talk about is gymnastics."

"At least I'm not so mad all the time! You're gonna scare her away!" Addy looked up at Dad for approval. "Right?"

Dad took the paper towels from me and finished wiping up the juice. "Addy, I'm amazed by your big, forgiving heart. That is definitely going to help when Mom comes home."

Addy smirked at me. "Told you, Maisy. Mom doesn't need you to be a jerk when she gets here."

Dad held up his hand. "I wasn't finished, Addy. Mom is fully aware that it might take a while for some of us to get used to being around her again."

"'Some of us' means Maisy, right, Dad?" Addy said, with her arms folded across her chest.

I rolled my eyes.

Dad put a hand on each of our shoulders and said, "You are the only two people who really understand what the other person is going through. Help each other get through this."

"I thought Mom wasn't coming home for a while," I said. "When she wrote me at camp, she said she was staying longer, and that she didn't want to come home till she was really ready."

"The sister facility in Boulder, Colorado, burned down in those awful wildfires. Mom offered her spot to someone who needed it more," Dad said.

"Someone who needs it more than Mom?" I asked.

Dad reached out and squeezed my hand. "Mom wouldn't be coming home if her doctor didn't think she was ready."

I pushed my chair back. "I'm gonna be late. I'll meet you guys in the car."

While I seethed about Mom, Addy spent the whole car ride talking about gymnastics. If I had to hear about her qualifying for level ten at the first meet one more time, I was going to lose my mind. As soon as Dad pulled up to school, I grabbed my backpack and hopped out of the Jeep.

"Wait, Mini," Dad called.

I turned around, waiting for him to say something, anything that would fix this. "What?"

"You forgot your breakfast." He passed my bagel to me. "I put a bottle of water in there, too."

"Thanks," I said, and ran into the building as the first bell rang.

The halls were empty because everyone else was already in homeroom. I threw the food in the garbage can near the front entrance and ran to my locker. I rushed through my combination, but the door wouldn't budge.

Convinced I did it too fast, I tried again slower. But it was still stuck.

"Was it four–twenty-eight–fourteen–thirty-five? Or did it start with twenty-eight?" My fingers tingled as I spun the lock around.

Panic set in as I realized I was going to be late for homeroom. It was only the third week of middle school, and I was going to get detention. Mom wasn't even home yet and she was already ruining my life.

I slid to the floor and sat against my locker.

Clark walked down the empty hallway and stopped in front of me. He leaned down to my level. "What's the matter? Did you forget your combination?"

"I wish that was my biggest problem," I mumbled.

"What?"

I tucked my hair behind my ears. "Never mind. I remember the four numbers, but not their order."

Clark whipped out his phone. "I made an app for that!"

"Of course you did," I said, feeling a smile sneak back on my face.

Clark slid his fingers across his phone screen. "Let's see if it actually works."

"I don't want to make you late," I said. "We both don't need to get detention."

Clark held up a pink slip of paper. "I have a late pass for helping Mr. Pembrook unfreeze his Smartboard. What're the numbers?"

"Four, twenty-eight, fourteen, thirty-five," I said. "But aren't there, like, a million combos?"

"Ten thousand," Clark said.

I slammed by body against my locker. "This is hopeless."

He must have been used to dealing with drama queens because he has a sister. He didn't even look at me like I was a freak; he just started entering numbers into his phone and trying different combinations while I hyperventilated.

The second bell rang.

"It's never going to work," I said.

Next thing I knew, he popped my locker open.

Instead of saying thank you like a normal person, I started crying, and not pretty crying, but the kind that involved snorts and phlegmy sounds.

"Um," Clark pushed his hair off his forehead. "Don't worry about the locker. I'll text you the combo."

I rubbed the back of my sleeve under my nose, like a totally disgusting person. "I'm sorry for acting so crazy. I'm having a weird morning."

I waited for Clark to walk away because I was breaking all the rules about seventh-grade boy–girl interactions. But he looked at me like it was no big deal that I was wiping snot off my face. He said,

"My house is the hot spot for weird mornings. I think it was built on a cosmic fault line or something."

He pulled a travel pack of tissues from the side pouch of his backpack and handed them to me.

"My mom's getting out of rehab this weekend," I said, the words tumbling out. I looked at the floor, letting my hair cover my face.

"Pills or alcohol?" Clark asked, like he was asking me if he could borrow a pen.

I peeked up through my wall of hair. "Uh, pills."

"My dad's an alcoholic. A recovering one, which means he did the whole in-patient treatment thing for three months. Now he goes to meetings every morning before work, and sometimes after work, too."

"What was it like when he came home?" I asked, in shock this conversation was actually happening. "Was it awkward?"

Clark pushed his hair back again. "Yeah, it was pretty uncomfortable for a while. My mom, my sister, and I had to get used to being around him again."

"That's what I'm worried about. My sister's acting like everything's normal, like our mom was just away on a work trip or something. But I'm still so . . ." I clenched my fists and ground my teeth.

"Mad?" finished Clark.

"Yeah." I breathed out really hard. "I'm the only one in my family who's not happy she's coming home. There must be something wrong with me."

"I broke my dad's CD collection when I found out he was coming home. He had at least forty Dave Matthews Band concert bootlegs from college. That case of CDs was his most prized possession and I broke every single one."

I sighed.

"There are meetings at Mapleton Congregational for kids like us. You should come with me."

"I haven't been to church in years, not since Mom stopped bringing us to Sunday school. What if I'm not allowed back?"

"You don't have to be Christian to go to the meetings. Our group is seriously a religious melting pot. We've got Muslims, Jewish kids, Hindus, pretty much every religion you can think of."

"What if there's no one else there like me?" I asked.

"Do you belong to a cult or something?" Clark teased.

I surprised myself by laughing. "No. I meant what if no one else's situation is as bad as mine?"

Clark's eyes looked sad. "You're going to fit right in. Meeting's after school. I'll meet you at your locker and we can cross the street together."

"Today?" I asked.

"Yeah. You got something better to do?" Clark asked.

CHAPTER TWELVE

BEA

"DON'T FORGET TO UPLOAD YOUR HOMEWORK TO THE PORTAL," Dr. Butterfield said, as the bell rang and everyone rushed to the door. "No sense doing all that work and not getting credit for it."

Maisy was waiting for me outside Dr. Butterfield's classroom. Her hair was styled into double dutch braids that were twisted into a bun at the nape of her neck. Her over-the-top hairstyle had to be a sign she was overwhelmed with anxiety.

"Sorry about this morning," Maisy said, without making eye contact.

I lowered my voice. "What's going on? Are you okay?"

Maisy gripped her books close to her chest and seemed to fold in on herself. Even her voice seemed smaller. "My mom's coming home this weekend."

"I thought she was going to stay longer," I said.

"Me too." Maisy started walking toward the cafeteria with her shoulders slumped and her feet dragging, while hordes of kids raced past her.

I reached out and put my hand on her arm. "Do you remember what you said to me when I found out my parents were getting divorced?" I asked.

Maisy groaned. "Probably something really dumb. We were so little when it happened."

"You actually said the perfect thing," I said.

"For real?" Maisy turned to me with wide eyes. "What did I say?"

"You said, 'I don't know what to say.'"

Maisy rolled her eyes. "I knew I said something dumb."

"It was exactly what I needed to hear." I shrugged my shoulders. "You were the only person who didn't pretend to have all the answers."

"That's 'cause I'm used to not knowing the right answers," Maisy said. "Especially in math."

"You told me that you didn't know what it felt like to have parents going through a divorce, so you didn't know what to say," I said. "Then you asked me what you could do to make me feel better."

Maisy put her finger on her lips, like she was thinking hard. "You wanted to have a sleepover with our My Little Pony dolls, my mom's monster cookies, and a binge session of *Austin & Ally.*"

"It was exactly what I needed," I said.

Maisy let out a long sigh. "If only watching *Austin & Ally* could fix this."

"I don't know what to say." I touched her arm again. "But I'll do whatever you want to help you get through this. I'm sorry I've been so wrapped up in my own stuff lately. But, I swear, I'm here for you."

"Thanks." Maisy smiled at me. "You would think I could talk to my own sister about this, but she's happy Mom's coming home. It's like she forgot all the crappy things Mom did before she left."

"Addy just wants your old mom back," I said.

"Well, that's not gonna happen," Maisy said. "And I'm not covering for her this time. So when she starts going back to her old ways . . ."

"What if she doesn't?"

"Yeah, right," Maisy said. "She always goes back on her promises."

"What if the treatment center really helped her? What if she's better?" I asked.

"You think I'm dumb enough to get my hopes up?" Maisy scrunched up her face. "Dad and Addy are going to be all heartbroken and shocked when Mom starts pulling the same garbage. But I'm going to be ready."

"But—" I started.

Maisy held up her hand. "You don't know what it's like to be in my situation. Remember?"

"Okay. Change of subject. We're all going to Mia's after school today," I said. "I promised the girls I would help with their science homework."

Maisy wrinkled up her face again. "I can't today. Can we do it tomorrow?"

"The girls need me to help today because their packet's due tomorrow. I *need* you there," I said.

"I just said I can't go." Maisy threw up her hands. "You don't really need me, anyway."

I could hear the desperation in my own voice, but I couldn't help it. "I still feel awkward around the M & Ms when you're not there. What are you doing that's so important?"

"I can't tell you," Maisy said.

I folded my arms across my chest. "What happened to no more secrets?"

"I just told you about my mom coming home. Isn't that enough?" Maisy said. "Why do I always have to prove myself to you?"

"I'm sorry," I said. "I haven't gotten my footing yet with the M & Ms. I still need you around in case things get awkward."

"Did you ever think that keeping my end of the pact might be harder than yours was? At least at camp, we weren't dealing with home and school drama. All you had to do was train me for the Amelia Cup," Maisy said.

"Like training you for the Amelia Cup was easy?" I said.

"That's all you had to focus on." Maisy held up one finger while she stared me down. "That one thing."

I shook my head. "Did you ever think that my stakes are higher than yours? If I couldn't come through with my end of the pact, worse case you would be miserable at camp for six weeks. If your end of the pact doesn't work, I'm going to be a loser for the rest of middle school and most likely high school."

"You have me, and we're going to make this work. Just remember, I can't live this pact twenty-four-seven, like we did at camp." Maisy put her hand on my arm. "And neither can you."

MAISY

When the last bell rang, Clark was leaning against my locker reading a worn-out paperback book that had two creepy aliens on the cover.

"So glad I'm not in honors English." I popped my locker open, feeling a little silly about how I panicked when I couldn't open it that morning. "Sci-fi is my most hated genre."

Clark closed the ratty book and shoved it in his backpack. "I'm not reading it for school."

"You're reading *The Martian Chronicles* for fun?" I shoved some books in my locker and pulled out the notebooks, binders, and text-books I needed for homework.

Clark shrugged. "I bought a big cardboard box of used books for two bucks at the library sale. Griffin and Marshall bet me I can't read them all by Christmas."

I shoved all my stuff in my backpack and swung it on my back. "What happens if you lose?"

Clark headed toward the back exit. I was relieved no one would see us together and start asking questions about where we were going.

"They get to pick our Comic-Con costumes," Clark said.

"You get to pick the costumes if you win?" I followed Clark out the door into the sunshine.

"Exactly," Clark said. "They're threatening to make me dress up like Mystique from X-Men for Halloween."

"I could see your motivation," I said. We approached the cross-walk between the school and Mapleton Congregational Church, and my heart started pounding.

I didn't even realize I had stopped short until Clark said, "What's the matter? Is it your backpack? That thing looks like it weighs more than you."

"I'm a lot stronger than I look." I hitched my backpack higher. "My bunk won this really big tournament at camp this summer."

"Guess you don't need me to carry your bag then," Clark said.

"Nope. I'm all set." I started walking again. "I just feel weird about this group thing."

"I didn't want to go my first time; my mom forced me, but I ended up liking it," Clark said, while we waited for the walk signal to light up.

"The first time I met my camp therapist, Dr. Beth, I thought she was a complete freak. She looks like a hippie, has, like, a hundred rescue cats, and she lives on McDonald's and Taco Bell. But she turned out to be pretty cool," I said as we crossed the street.

"Wait till you meet Pastor Bob," Clark said.

As we walked up the church steps, it felt weird to be wearing regular school clothes instead of the ironed dresses Mom used to make us wear to Sunday school.

"Are you sure it's okay we're not dressed nice?" I asked, smoothing down my leggings. I hadn't realized that morning I had grabbed the ones with the hole in them.

Clark laughed. "You're fine. Wait till you see what Pastor Bob's wearing."

I followed Clark down the hall and into the church's gym, which smelled like fresh-baked cookies and sweaty kids. There were metal chairs set up in a circle, but no one was sitting. Kids were shooting hoops into an ancient basketball net, and other kids were sitting on the ground surrounded by textbooks and notebooks. I spotted Pepper Johnson, who I knew from summer theater, and Stephen Patrick, who went to preschool with Bea and me before transferring to the private boys' school across the river. I always thought they were normal. But I guess everyone thought I was normal, too.

There was only one grown-up in the room, but he didn't look like a pastor. He wore a black denim shirt with the sleeves rolled up, showing his tattoo-covered forearms. He had a goatee and was wearing black jeans and short black leather boots.

"What's up, Pastor Bob?" Clark called.

"Hey! What's up, Clark?" He gave Clark a fist bump. "What's your mom been feeding you, man? You shot up at least a foot this summer!"

Clark laughed. "Maybe I can actually take you on in basketball now."

Pastor Bob smirked. "You know I'm MVP of the Holy Hoopsters."

"Must be stiff competition on a basketball team full of pastors," Clark said.

"You should see Pastor Mike's jump shot," Pastor Bob said.

Clark laughed. Then he waved his hand toward me. "This is my friend Maisy."

Pastor Bob reached out his tattooed and silver ring–covered hand to shake mine. I shook his hand. It was warm and he didn't squeeze my hand too tight, which made me instantly like him.

"Hope you're both hungry. I made my famous chocolate chip sea salt cookies," Pastor Bob said. "Gluten-free and nut-free, but not—"

"Taste-free," finished Clark.

"You got it," Pastor Bob said. "Show our new friend to the cookie department and then do me a favor and find a seat 'cause no one ever wants to sit down first."

I followed Clark to a card table that was filled with plates of cookies that had the perfect chocolate-chip-to-dough ratio. I watched as Clark popped a cookie into his mouth and pretty much swallowed it whole.

I laughed. "I always thought my sister Addy eats like a twelve-year-old boy. Totally confirmed now."

Clark swallowed hard and loaded up a plate with cookies and handed it to me. "It's impossible not to eat these in one bite."

Pastor Bob called out, "Come on, everyone. Grab some of my famous cookies and sit down."

Clark grabbed us two seats right in the middle of the circle of chairs, which made me feel like everyone was staring at me. I counted the kids as they took their seats and realized there were eight other kids besides me and Clark who had messed-up family situations.

Pastor Bob sat down. "Hey, friends. Happy everyone's back from summer vacation. Missed you guys."

All the kids cheered in a kind of ironic way, but you could tell they were glad to be there.

Pastor Bob said, "What's the first rule of group?"

"What happens in group *stays* in group," everyone chanted back.

I normally have an inner eye roll moment when adults say things like this. But if these kids had as much practice keeping secrets as I did, then maybe they would keep their mouths shut. Maybe I could finally talk to other people who could really understand why I was so mad at Mom.

Pastor Bob clapped his hands together and his chunky silver rings made a ringing sound as they smacked together. "Let's hear rose and thorn of summer vacay."

Then he pulled a dirty-looking hacky sack from his back pocket and tossed it to Pepper.

Pepper tucked her thick black hair behind her ear. "Rose was definitely Disney. We went with my mom, Grandma, and little cousins."

Pastor Bob nodded. "Who doesn't love some Mickey Mouse?"

There were some cheers and goofy *woot-woot* sounds. Then Pastor Bob cut in. "And what was the thorn?"

Pepper started picking at the frayed edges of a hole in her jeans. "Dad finally moved out. I thought I would be glad, but it's been kind of weird since he left."

If Mom moved out, I would consider that a rose, not a thorn.

Pastor Bob breathed in deep and said, "That really sucks, Pepper. Tell us some more about it."

I didn't know if I would ever be able to talk about my situation, but I had to admit it felt pretty good to hear someone else talk about theirs.

CHAPTER THIRTEEN

BEA

"SEE HOW THE CONTINENTS FIT TOGETHER LIKE PUZZLE PIECES?"
I said, pointing to the diagram of the continents on Mia's science
packet. "That's because they used to be part of one big land mass
made up of Africa, India, South America, Antarctica, and Australia."

Mia looked up from her phone and nodded.

Meghan was putting more focus into picking off her nail polish
than she was on the packet.

"The continents rest on tectonic plates, which are constantly
moving," I continued, changing up my tone to sound more exciting.
"When the tectonic plates moved, the continents did too."

"So the answer is tectonic plates?" Meghan said.

"Wait . . . no. That was just the explanation that went with the
answer. So you understand the concept," I said.

Mia scrolled though her phone. "Don't worry about us under-standing it. Just give us the answers so we can get this done."

"Um. Okay." I pulled out a notebook and started jotting down the long response in big letters, so all the girls could see. When I was finished, I pushed the notebook in the middle of Mia's dining room table, next to the big bowl of popcorn her mom had made for us.

All the girls except Madeline huddled around my notebook and scribbled my answer in their Earth Science packets.

Looking up from her copy of *The Crucible,* Madeline said, "You guys better be careful. If all your answers look the same, you can get an honor code violation."

"Easy for you to say," Mia said, while she quickly scribbled my answers in her own packet. "You're good at school."

"My mom already warned me that I'm going to get my phone taken away if I get another bad homework grade," Meghan said.

"The portal's the worst," Madison said. "My mom knows my grades before I do."

Chloe groaned. "The portal sucks."

"My mom never checks the portal," I said, while I wrote out the next answer.

"What?" Mia asked.

"She just asks me how I'm doing in school," I said.

"You're so lucky," Meghan said.

"Can she talk to my mom?" Madison asked. "Her whole life revolves around how me and my brother do in school."

I always felt like Mom's life revolved around me, but in a good way. Like when I was at school, she worked, but when I was home it was all about me and her. Lately, it's been about me, her, and Mr. Pembrook. He's been over almost every night for dinner since I got back from camp, and the only time I have Mom to myself is when we're both rushing to get out the door in the morning.

While the girls copied my answers, I opened my own math book and got ready to answer the first word problem.

Maple Rivers has 64 streets and 1,340 households. Guess the number of males living on a street if the average family size is four people.

I blinked twice. I read the problem again. I was used to whipping through math problems. Using basic formulas to compute simple answers. But seventh-grade math was different. For once, I didn't know how to even get started solving the problem.

"Bea? Helloooooo," Mia said.

I looked up from my textbook and unclenched my teeth from my pencil. "Sorry, did you say something?"

"We finished the packet. Should we do social studies or math next?" Mia asked.

I slid my textbook toward her. "You guys wouldn't be working on problems like this, would you?"

Meghan laughed. "Um, no, thank God."

"We're still reviewing stuff from last year," Madison said.

The girls stuffed their science packets into their folders and pulled out math review packets.

"We're gonna need a lot of help with this," Meghan said. "I spent the whole summer blocking out school. I don't remember how to do any of this."

Mia picked up her phone and started texting someone. She waited for a response, which was apparently from her mom who was two rooms away from us. "My mom said you guys can stay for dinner so we can get all of our work done."

I closed my own math book and put it in my bag.

"You can stay to help us, right, Bea?" Mia begged.

"Of course. I'll stay as long as you guys need."

MAISY

I WAS READY TO GO HOME AS SOON AS THE MEETING ENDED. I hadn't shared anything, but hearing everyone else talk about sad stuff made me feel like I needed a nap. But Clark stayed behind to help put the metal folding chairs away. I felt like I had to stay and help him because I wouldn't have gone to the meeting if it wasn't for him.

Clark picked up a metal chair and gave it a little bump and it folded in half. He made it look easy. I tried the same exact thing and, of course, nothing; it didn't work for me.

"Hey, Maisy," Pastor Bob said. "Why don't you leave the chairs to the big guy? You can help clean up the food table."

"Okay," I said.

"Save me some cookies," Clark said, while he put a metal chair on top of the stack.

"OMG! How are you still hungry?" I asked. "You already ate a million cookies."

Pastor Bob handed me a box of Ziploc bags. "Give him a break. Growing two feet in one summer must make a guy hungry."

"Do you want chocolate chip or oatmeal butterscotch?" I asked.

"Yes!" said Clark.

I laughed and started filling a bag with cookies.

Pastor Bob grabbed the stack of paper plates and put them on a metal cart, next to a pile of napkins. He shook his head. "I don't know why I put the plates and napkins out every week. No one ever uses them. You middle schoolers eat like a pack of wolves."

"It's your fault," Clark said. "Your cookies are so good, no one's got time for a plate."

Pastor Bob laughed. "You gonna come back next time, Maisy? Or did we scare you away?"

I thought about Stephen Patrick sharing that story about how his school principal called the police last year when his mom showed up to the carpool line drunk. He made it look so easy to share. But I didn't think I would ever be able to talk about the stuff Mom did.

Before I could answer, Clark walked over and grabbed his bag of cookies from me. He took a big bite of an oatmeal cookie and said with his mouth full, "Yeah, she's coming back with me next time."

"Uh, okay," I said, while giving Clark a *What the heck?* look.

"Awesome!" Pastor Bob said. "Catch you guys later. I have to get ready for Holy Hoopsters practice. My jump shot could use a little work if we want to make the playoffs."

As soon as Pastor Bob left the room, I hissed, "Why did you say I was coming back? I'm *never* gonna be able to tell everyone my business like these kids do."

"Pastor Bob didn't say anything about talking. He just asked if you were coming," Clark said.

"You have a little . . ." I pointed to the side of my mouth.

Clark wiped his mouth with the back of his hand, but there was still an oatmeal crumble sticking to the side of his mouth. I stood on my tiptoes and covered the palm of my hand with my sweatshirt sleeve. Then I wiped off the crumb.

"There. That was gonna drive me crazy," I said. "I just don't know if I'm a group type person."

"Says the girl whose friend group has an actual name," Clark said, while he swung his backpack onto his back.

"That's different," I said, grabbing my own bag. "Besides, I'm not the one who gave us a name. That was Mia."

"Give it a chance," Clark said. "That's all I'm saying."

I breathed out hard. "I don't know. The meeting was okay, I guess. I just feel kind of weird now after hearing all that stuff."

Clark looked at me. "Your mom's coming home this weekend, right?"

I looked down at the ground and nodded.

"Trust me," Clark said. "Come to the next meeting."

CHAPTER FOURTEEN

BEA

"BEA?" MOM SMOOTHED MY HAIR BACK AND SPOKE IN A GENTLE TONE. "Bea? You need to wake up, sweetie. Monica's going to be here soon."

I opened my eyes and pulled my cheek from the puddle of drool on my math book. "It's Saturday?"

Mom nodded slowly, her eyes wide.

"No! It can't be Saturday! I never submitted my math homework last night," I said.

The deep V Mom gets when she's worried appeared between her eyebrows. "You've been up late every night this week doing homework. Maybe you're taking too many honors classes."

If only Mom knew the reason I was up late doing my own homework was because I had spent every afternoon at Mia's house for the past week doing the M & Ms' homework for them.

"It's fine," I said, on my way to the bathroom. "I'll submit it today. Then I'll email Dr. Butterfield and say our internet was down last night."

"I think . . ." Mom paused at the bathroom door. "You've never lied to a teacher before. Maybe you're spending too much time with these girls."

I squeezed a thick line of bright blue toothpaste on my toothbrush. "So you want me to have a perfect GPA, but no friends, like last year?"

"Why does it have to be one or the other?" Mom sighed. "Just try to balance your time so your only focus isn't climbing the social ladder."

"Okay, Mom." I shoved my toothbrush in my mouth to signal the conversation was over.

I washed up and rushed back to my room to email Dr. Butterfield and get dressed. I had only spent time with Peyton and Vivi twice before, and both times I was wearing the wrong thing. The first time I met them, I wore my brand-new jeans and a sparkly sweatshirt with booties—my version of dressing up. But Peyton and Vivi were both wearing leggings and T-shirts. The next time I saw them, I dressed down in my soccer shorts and a T-shirt, and of course they were both wearing dresses.

This time, though, I didn't have to stress about what to wear because Monica had mailed me a package with a cream sundress, a jean jacket, and gold flats with a note about a special outfit for our special girls' day. I threw it on and admired myself in the mirror.

I walked into the kitchen just as Maisy threw open our back door.

She whistled, and said, "You clean up nice."

"Thanks," I said. "But what're you doing here? Isn't your mom coming home today?"

"Exactly." Maisy reached her hand into the open box of granola on the table and popped a bunch in her mouth.

"Won't your dad be mad when he finds out you left?" I asked.

Maisy shrugged. "He's so happy Mom's coming home, he won't even notice I'm not there."

Mom walked in the kitchen and poured herself a cup of coffee. "I don't know about that, Maisy."

"Mom, please can Maisy come with me today?" I asked. I was exhausted from a week of being my best self for the M & Ms. I could use a buffer between me and my perfect stepfamily.

Mom sighed. "It's not up to me."

Maisy clapped her hands together and her face broke into a huge smile. "I have a plan that Monica will have to say yes to!"

"Of course you do," I said, a smile sneaking onto my face.

"I can be Monica's social media photographer! I'll take pictures of you guys all day for her Instagram story. She would have to say yes to that, right?" Maisy turned to look at Mom and me with desperate eyes.

"It's fine with me, as long as Monica's okay with it," Mom said.

Maisy smiled. "I am *so* good at taking social media pics. It's a natural talent of mine."

I groaned. "Now the pressure is really on to look perfect. Maisy, come help me flat-iron my hair."

"You look great," Maisy said.

"Maybe for a regular shopping day, but not for an Instagram account with half a million followers," I said.

My phone lit up with a text from Monica.

I groaned again. "They're already here."

Mom kissed the top of my head. "You look beautiful. Have a good time and try to get to know Monica and the girls a little better."

I used both hands to smooth my hair down.

Monica honked her horn.

"Come on," Maisy said. "Let's go do this."

Monica was sitting in our driveway in a shiny new white mini-van. If she was surprised that I was walking to her car with Maisy in tow, she didn't show it.

"What happened to your Mini Cooper?" I asked.

"What happened to your curls?" she asked, at the exact same time.

We both laughed.

Maisy jumped in. "I gave her a keratin treatment. Doesn't it look great?"

Monica smiled. "You look fabulous, Bea!" And turning to Maisy, said "You must be Maisy."

I realized then that Dad had actually been listening when we talked on the phone the other night and I told him I was hanging out with Maisy again. Peyton and Vivi were so loud in the background that I didn't think he really heard what I was saying.

Maisy started right in on her pitch. "I'm an amazing photographer. All my friends ask me to edit their photos. Bea knows today's a really special day for you guys, so she thought it would be nice if I came to take pictures all day for your Instagram story."

"What a great idea, right, girls?" Monica turned to the back.

Vivi beamed a wide smile. "Yeah, good idea."

Peyton gave her sister the look of death.

"If you can take pictures half as good as you can style hair, then it's a win-win," Monica continued. Then she turned toward me. "I told your dad we needed a bigger car for our bigger family," Monica said.

My stomach sank. "You're preg—" I started.

"No, silly." Monica laughed. "We need room for all three of our girls, and their friends," she said. "Watch this. I just press this button on the remote and the door opens."

The side door slid open, revealing Peyton and Vivi sitting in the white leather bucket seats, each wearing a cream sundress with a jean jacket and gold flats. When I got a closer look at Monica, I could see she was wearing an adult-sized version of the same outfit. I knew this day was about more than just a curated Instagram post for Monica. I knew she was trying her best to include me. But when you put three girls in the same outfit, it's easy to see who doesn't belong.

MAISY

You could tell Monica was a pretty big deal because Sheila, the sales lady at Posh Petticoats Bridal Boutique, brought us a silver tray of nonalcoholic mimosas, fancy pink macarons, and chocolate-covered strawberries. I took a picture of it and added it to the @morethanmomjeans story. I also took a picture of the girls and Monica toasting with the mimosas, and another one of the girls eating the macarons.

Bea and I were holed up in a dressing room that was almost as big as my bedroom. I sat in a fancy gold and white chair with Monica's phone and added a filter to the artsy picture I had taken of a pile of wedding veils.

Bea held up the bridesmaid dress in front of her, with her eyes wide. "It's not that bad, right?" she whispered.

"But you hate hot pink," I hissed. "Not to be mean, but I can see why. It clashes with your hair."

Bea whispered. "But *Monica* loves hot pink."

"That's 'cause she's not a redhead," I said.

"Neither are her daughters," Bea hissed.

"There are so many other colors that look good on both blonds and redheads," I whispered.

Bea kicked off her gold flats and pulled her sundress off over her head. "So I should tell Monica to pick a different theme color for her wedding just because I don't look good in it?"

"I'm just saying . . ." I started.

Bea stepped into the dress. "I want to spend more time with my dad. Ruining his fiancée's wedding plans isn't going to make that happen. Now help me zip this up."

I couldn't help cringing while I zipped up the back of Bea's dress. The hot pink fabric made every single one of Bea's freckles jump out from her pale skin and her hair look neon orange.

Bea turned around slowly with both hands holding up the top of her dress and a hopeful smile. "What do you think?" she asked.

Monica apparently didn't know that strapless dresses only work with people who have something to hold the dress up.

"Um, what happens when you let go?" I asked.

Bea let her hands drop to her sides. The waist was tight enough so the dress didn't fall down, but the empty top of the dress stayed out in the shape of boobs, and you could see her black sports bra lying flat underneath.

"Um, maybe they have the same dress, but with straps," I said. "And in a different color."

Bea raised her eyebrows. "Anything else?"

"It should be shorter, too, because you know you're gonna trip," I said.

"Girls, come on out. Let's see how you look," Monica called.

Bea covered her face with her hands, then peeked between her fingers at me.

"There's no way Peyton and Vivi will look good in their dresses either," I whispered. "Monica will *have* to pick a different one."

Bea nodded. Her lips were stuck together in a flat line. She took a deep breath and opened her dressing room door slowly. I gave her a nudge, and she turned around and gave me a dirty look before stepping forward.

Sheila waved Bea over to the podium in front of the floor-to-ceiling mirrors. Bea made it two steps forward before tripping over the bottom of the dress.

"Don't worry," Sheila said. "As soon as you throw on a pair of heels, the length will be perfect."

Bea waited till Sheila turned around, then looked at me and mouthed "Heels?!"

Peyton's dressing room door opened and I wanted to cry for Bea, because her future stepsister looked like a supermodel in the ugliest bridesmaid dress ever. It fit her the way it was supposed to, and her blond hair and golden skin were made for hot pink.

The saleslady gasped. "This dress is perfect for you! Can I take a picture of you for our Instagram?"

Peyton shrugged, like it was no big deal, like people were always asking her to pose for pictures. "Sure."

Bea took a step back, so she was out of the shot. I caught her eye and hoped she got my secret message: *I know this totally sucks.*

"Let's show the girls how great you look," Monica said, while she walked out of Vivi's dressing room.

Since Vivi was younger, her dress was cut differently, so she didn't have the fit issues Bea did, and of course hot pink was her color.

Vivi ran over to Bea and Peyton with a huge smile. "We're twinning!"

But it was more like a game of "Who doesn't belong here?"

Monica gasped, and I was so relieved that she saw what a disaster this was. She would have to pick a different dress now that she saw just how bad Bea looked next to her daughters.

But Monica said, "Girls! You all look beautiful!"

She turned to Sheila with her hands clasped tight. "Don't they all look gorgeous?"

Sheila, who was probably adding up the price tags in her head, nodded and said, "Breathtaking!"

Bea put her hands across her chest. "Um, Peyton and Vivi look amazing. But me, not so much."

"What are you talking about, Bea? You look like the beautiful redhead in that John William Waterhouse painting," Monica said. "I would kill for your gorgeous hair."

The suspicious side of me thought Monica was just saying that because *her* daughters looked amazing in the dresses, and she wanted all the girls to wear the same thing. But from what I had seen of Monica so far, I think she genuinely thought Bea looked great in the dress, which was even worse, because Bea would never want to hurt her feelings.

"Maisy, you need to take a pic of these beautiful girls so I can post!" Monica said.

Bea looked at me with wild "rescue me" eyes.

"Um. Don't you want to surprise Bea's dad? If he sees it on your Instagram, you'll ruin it," I said.

"Good point." Monica took her phone back from me.

Bea shot me a grateful smile.

"Now, let's get those dresses off so I can pay for them," Monica said.

Bea and I went back in her dressing room and shut the door behind us.

Bea looked in the mirror. "It's not that bad, is it?"

I tried to sound hopeful. "Maybe it will fit better after you get it altered. You should see how my Grandma looks in dresses off the rack. Everything is gigantic on her and she looks ridiculous. But then she gets the dresses altered and she looks amazing."

Bea wrinkled her nose. "All the alterations in the world won't make me look any better in this color."

We could hear Monica's and Sheila's voices coming from the front of the store.

"These dresses are all final sale," Sheila said. "Once you pay for them, I start the alterations right away."

I started whipping my fingers through my hair, but for once braiding wasn't doing anything to soothe my nerves. This was big.

"I wouldn't dream of returning them," Monica said. "The girls all looked like princesses."

"I look more like the Frog Prince," Bea mumbled.

"This is it. This is your chance to speak up before Monica pays for the dresses," I said.

Bea took one last look at herself in the mirror before taking off her dress. She draped it over her dressing room door.

"Here you go, Monica. It's all ready for you to pay for it," Bea said.

I sighed. "No, Bea. Don't do this."

Bea pulled her shirt overhead without saying a word.

Monica called, "Hope you girls are hungry. I made reservations at that fancy sushi place on Sugar Maple Boulevard."

I put my finger down my throat and pretended to gag, since Bea hates sushi more than anything in the world. It's literally the only food she won't eat.

"Can't wait!" Bea called out.

I looked Bea in the eyes. "Your mom told you to get to know Monica and the girls today. But maybe you really need to let them get to know you."

CHAPTER FIFTEEN

BEA

MONICA'S FAVORITE NINETIES HIP-HOP MUSIC BLASTED FROM THE minivan's speakers and she rapped along while Vivi filmed for the @morethanmomjeans story. I thought about all the times Mom and Dad fought over the car radio station. Dad knows the words to every rap song that came out between 1985 and 2000, while Mom calls herself an old soul because she loves Fleetwood Mac and the Grateful Dead. I was glad Dad had found someone who had more in common with him, but I felt weird rooting for him and Monica, like I was somehow betraying Mom.

Peyton held up her phone. "Look! I'm on the Posh Petticoats Instagram."

Vivi grabbed her phone. "You look sooo pretty."

Monica pulled into a parking spot on Sugar Maple Boulevard. "Let me see," she said.

Vivi unclicked her seat belt and climbed up front with Peyton's phone.

Monica sighed and put her hand over her mouth. "Oh, Pey. You look gorgeous."

There had to be an ugly stepsister in every story; in this story it was clearly me.

As soon as Monica put the car in park, we heard a sharp knock on her window.

She opened her car door and screeched at the top of her lungs. "Jimmy! You scared me! What are you doing here?"

I watched through the window as Dad swept Monica up in his arms and said, "I missed my girls too much to stay away. Plus, you know how much I love eating at Bento."

I knew I wasn't a part of "the girls" Dad couldn't be away from for a few hours because I hadn't seen him since before I left for camp.

Monica hit the car remote and the van door opened. Vivi literally jumped out of the car and into Dad's arms like she hadn't seen him in months, screaming, "Jim-Dad!"

Maisy raised her eyebrow and mouthed, "Jim-Dad?"

Peyton hopped out next and gave Dad a high five. "Hey, Jim-Dad."

Maisy and I looked at each other without blinking. I was glad she was there with me. Otherwise, I don't know if I would've been able to get out of the car and face "Jim-Dad."

Dad poked his face into the minivan and asked, "Where's my girl?"

I couldn't move. It felt like I was glued to the leather seat. Then I felt Maisy's hand on my back giving me a gentle nudge.

I pulled myself up off the seat and climbed out of the car and forced myself to sound cheery. "Hey, Dad."

Turns out I wasn't the only one who had gone through a makeover. Dad was wearing dark-rinse cuffed and fitted jeans, a lumberjack-style flannel, and slip-on sneakers like the boys at school wore. This only solidified my feeling that you can't be a member of his new family unit without looking fabulous. He was going to be mortified when I stood next to his perfect new family at the wedding.

"Love your hair," Dad said, while leaning in to kiss me.

His new beard felt scratchy across my face, and he smelled like hair pomade and cologne, which made me feel like a stranger was kissing my cheek.

"Thanks," I said, smoothing it down.

Maisy hopped out of the minivan. "Hey, Jimmy. Long time, no see."

Dad smiled and gave Maisy a fist bump. "I haven't seen you

since you and Bea were obsessed with My Little Pony. Remember you guys used to bring them everywhere?"

Maisy laughed and held up her phone. "Now we bring these everywhere."

Monica cut in. "Good thing Maisy came. She's been taking pictures all day for Instagram."

"Takes the pressure off me." Dad pretended to wipe sweat off his brow. "Being an Instagram boyfriend can be very stressful."

"Can you get one of all of us?" Monica handed her phone to Maisy.

Maisy waved her hands at us. "Get on the edge of the sidewalk so we get a little bit of the restaurant window but you can still see the downtown buildings behind you."

"Let me know when you're old enough for a job," Monica said. "I could use a photographer like you on staff."

Monica, Dad, and the girls moved together in one solid pack, like they were used to taking family pictures together all the time. But I didn't know where to be. Did I stand with Peyton and Vivi, my new almost stepsisters who flanked Dad's sides like they owned him? Or did I stand next to Dad, whose arm was wrapped firmly around Monica's waist?

Suddenly, I felt a hand reach for me.

"Come stand next to me, Bea," Monica said.

She was making it really hard not to like her.

We all smiled while Maisy took picture after picture. No one complained about how long it was taking, not even Dad, who used to give Mom a hard time whenever she even mentioned a family photo. If Monica could influence Dad to change this much, what was going to happen to Mom if she stayed with Mr. Pembrook?

"Did you get a good one?" Monica asked.

Maisy held up a thumbs-up.

Dad smacked his hands together and started walking toward the restaurant. "Let's eat."

"Can we get the sashimi special, a number four, and the combo platter?" Vivi said, following so close behind Dad, it looked like she was going to walk right into him.

Peyton looked up from her phone. "Let's also get the number eight and some of that Negi Yellowtail."

Monica put her hands to her chest and breathed in deep. "That was so good last time."

Dad held the door open for all of us.

"Me and Bea will have the California roll or anything else that isn't still alive," Maisy said, while we followed them through the door. "Maybe there's some chicken teriyaki or something on the menu?"

"Very funny, Maisy," I said, a bit too loud. "You know how much I *love* sushi. The yellowtail sounds great."

Maisy squeezed my arm.

The smell of raw fish hit me as soon as we walked into the

restaurant. I averted my eyes from the sushi bar where the chefs were working.

A woman with a jaw-grazing black bob ran over to Monica. "We've been getting so many reservations since you posted us on your story!"

Monica waved her hand like it was no big deal. "Are you kidding me? You know how much we love you guys."

The hostess smiled. "You are so sweet. I saved your usual table." Then she looked at Maisy and me. "I'll just add two chairs at the end."

I watched a waiter drag a chair from a neighboring table and add it to the end of an oval table. I was always going to be the extra chair at the end of Dad's new family.

MAISY

As Monica turned on Maple Drive, I probably looked as green as Bea had since she ate that salmon roll. I would rather go to school in the ugliest bridesmaid dress ever than to go home where Mom was waiting.

"Which house is yours, Maisy?" Monica asked.

"The white one with the black shutters," I said, wishing Monica drove slower.

"So you live in the house with the amazing garden," Monica said, like I was the luckiest person in town.

Bea squeezed my knee.

Monica pulled into my driveway, and my stomach instantly turned to Jell-O. I reached up to braid my hair, then remembered I had already used my nervous energy to put it in two braids.

"Thanks for being such a great photographer today," Monica said.

"Thanks for letting me come," I said. "And for lunch."

"Maybe next time we'll get you to try some sushi," Monica said, as the minivan door opened.

Bea looked like she was going to throw up. I gave her a sympathy smile and got out of the car.

I got to the front door and waved. I didn't want to go in, but Monica sat in front of the house waiting to make sure I got in okay. Bea gave me a thumbs-up and a big "It's gonna be okay smile" from the window.

I took a deep breath and turned the doorknob. I slipped my sandals off and lined them up next to the door. My breath caught in my chest. Mom's favorite shoes, her navy retro New Balance sneakers, size six and a half, were lined up next to Dad's work loafers. It was like she had never left.

I could hear voices coming from the kitchen. I debated sneaking up to my room, but I knew I would have to see Mom sooner or later. Pastor Bob said that sometimes the anticipation of something is worse than the real thing, so I walked toward the kitchen before I could talk myself out of it.

"And then, my roommate said—"

Mom froze midsentence when she saw me.

I braced myself for an uncomfortable hug, but Mom stayed where she was.

"Hi, Maisy," she said.

She looked different, not like the skinny mess she was when she left, but not like her old self who was styled from her hair down to the matching booties. This mom was somewhere in between the other two moms. Her hair was cut so it fell right at her shoulders, and it was air dried and wavy. She was wearing a simple black long-sleeved tee with boyfriend jeans, which showed she was back to a normal weight. She looked more comfortable than I had seen her in a long time. But that didn't mean she was really ready to be home.

I lifted my hand in a half wave. "Hi."

Grandma dug her knuckle in my back. "Go give your mom a hug."

Mom waved her hand, pretending to be casual, when I knew it had to be killing her that I wouldn't go anywhere near her. "It's fine, Raisa."

"Mom was just telling us about her roommate, Peggy," Dad said. "She's from North Dakota and she has five kids."

I wondered if Peggy from North Dakota had almost driven into a river with her kids in the car. I could feel my eyes shooting daggers at Mom.

Addy gave me a dirty look and said, "Mom, can you come to practice tomorrow? Wait until you see what I can do now!"

Mom sighed. "I'm sorry, sweetie, but I can't. I have outpatient treatment. Now that you have practice during the day . . ." Mom trailed off.

Addy kept her voice super cheery. "That's okay, Mom. I'm just glad you made it home in time for my first meet."

Mom had only been home for a few hours and she was already letting Addy down, and Addy was already forgiving her.

"I wouldn't miss it," Mom said. "Maybe it's better that I don't see you in practice so I'm surprised at the meet."

Grandma put her hand on Addy's shoulder. "So much better to surprise your mom."

Dad nodded. "It will be more special that way."

It was like I was the only person in the room who knew there was no way Mom was making it to the meet. By the time Addy's meet rolled around, Mom would be back in her room with Peggy.

Grandma turned to me. "How was dress shopping?"

I shrugged. "Bea's dress doesn't fit her right and it's the wrong color."

"I can't do anything about the color," Mom said. "But if Bea needs any alterations, I can do it for her."

Like I would let Mom anywhere near Bea's dress?

"She's all set," I said. "I need to go do my homework."

I waited for Mom to talk me into staying in the kitchen longer, but she said, "Okay."

As I walked away, Dad said in a hushed tone, "She just needs some time."

Of course Addy piped in. "Hasn't she had enough already?"

I ran up the stairs and as soon as I got in my room, I shut the door behind me. I breathed in and counted to five, like Dr. Beth taught me. Then I breathed out for five seconds. But it didn't loosen up that tight feeling in my chest. I stretched my arms to the ceiling and tried to clear all of the thoughts swirling around in my mind. The worst part of anxiety is that I can never turn my brain off.

Addy threw the door open and barged in the room. "I can't believe you wouldn't hug your own mom. You are literally the meanest person in the world."

I kicked her pile of dirty leotards and sweats. "At least I'm not the messiest person in the world."

Addy snatched up her pile of clothes and stuffed them in the hamper. "I can be neat sometimes. Can you ever not be mean?"

I grabbed my pajamas from my drawer, making a point to pull it out all the way, so Addy could see how neat it was. "At least when Mom screws up, I'll be ready for it."

CHAPTER SIXTEEN

BEA

MAISY WALKED INTO MY ROOM MUNCHING ON ONE OF MOM'S homemade oatmeal raisin breakfast cookies. Since her mom came home, she gets out of her house as fast as she can in the mornings, sometimes getting to my house before I'm even dressed for school.

"Wait a second," I said, as I uploaded my English paper to the portal.

"Is that for Mrs. Heart's class?" Maisy sunk down onto my bed with her backpack on, half a cookie stuffed in her mouth and another in her hand.

I snapped my laptop shut. "Yes."

She brushed the cookie crumbs off her legs and onto my bedspread. "Did she give the honors kids a different due date for *The Crucible* paper? Mine was due yesterday by five p.m."

"Mine was too," I said, trying not to sound as stressed out as I felt. "I lost ten points for turning it in late. But if the paper's good enough I can still get a ninety."

"If you weren't so busy doing all of Mia's homework, you wouldn't have to turn your own stuff in late," Maisy said. "Didn't you turn in your science packet late, too?"

I sighed, "Yeah, but—"

"Seriously, Bea. You can't keep up with the M & Ms' homework and yours," Maisy said.

I pulled my hair into a high ponytail and wrapped my Poppy Red scrunchie around it. "I can't tell Mia no. I don't want to give her any excuse not to keep me around."

Maisy scarfed down the other cookie. "You're the Genius Whisperer. As long as you keep the girls connected to Clark, you can back off on doing their homework. Seriously, talk to them about it today."

"Maybe they can save me for the really big assignments," I said. "The ones that they really need help with. But I don't know."

"Speaking of Clark, are you ever going to work with him on the robotics project?" Maisy asked. "He has some really good ideas, but he said you're never around to meet."

"I'm free on Wednesdays and Fridays after school because that's when Mia has ballet. But he's never free then, and neither are you, coincidentally. Are you ever going to tell me what you guys have been up to?" I asked.

"I would tell you if it was just about me," Maisy said. "But it's not fair for me to talk about Clark's stuff."

"You girls better leave or you'll be late," Mom called.

"I can give you guys a ride," Mr. Pembrook called.

Maisy raised an eyebrow while she stood up and hitched her bag back on her back.

"He slept over last night," I hissed, while I shoved my feet into my sneakers.

Maisy's jaw dropped and I could see bits of chewed up oatmeal cookie in her mouth.

"No, thanks," I called. "Um . . . We're trying to hit our ten thousand steps for the day."

"Do you even have a Fitbit?" Maisy said.

"Do you want to show up at school with the math teacher?" I challenged.

"He's actually pretty cool," Maisy said. "All the kids really like him. He stays in every lunch period for anyone who needs help."

"That doesn't mean they would want their mom dating him," I said. "Come on. We don't want to be late."

When we got to the flagpole, I could feel energy in the air, almost like a buzzing. It felt like something big was about to happen. All of the M & Ms were huddled up together over Mia's phone, whispering and nudging each other.

"Hey, guys," Maisy said, walking into the center of the huddle. "What's up?"

Mia put her hand to her chest in a dreamy way, looked to the heavens, and said, "Terrance Millstone."

Maisy got right to the point. "What about him?"

"Isn't he living in Tokyo for his dad's work?" I asked.

"Not anymore!" Mia said, practically waving jazz hands at us.

"He's back," Madison chimed in.

"His dad got transferred back to the Manhattan office," Chloe added, with a smug smile. "He lives next door to me. That's how I know."

Mia spoke in slow motion, emphasizing every syllable. "That's also how Chloe got us the scoop on the new Mapleton Middle School Glow Up of the Year!"

"What?" I said. The ground felt like it was going to swallow me whole. I had been so busy helping the girls with their homework, I had all but abandoned my Genius Whisperer duties. This was all my fault.

"What about Clark?" Maisy asked, slowly, like she was scared of the answer.

Madeline reached over and grabbed a Frappuccino out of Madison's hand and took a big sip. "Terrance is *way* hotter than Clark," she said.

"And he's in all of our classes," Madison said, while she took her drink back from Madeline.

"And we don't need an interpreter to talk to him," Meghan added.

Maisy and I locked eyes. I was waiting for her to send me a signal not to panic, a sign that she was concocting a new plan on the spot. But she looked just as worried as I was. I could see it in the blank stare looking back at me. Maisy was out of backup plans.

"And he doesn't come with Griffin and Marshall," Mia said.

The girls burst out laughing, while Maisy and I forced out laughs.

Mia held up her phone. "Check him out."

All I could see was a blurry figure as I blinked back tears and tried to catch my breath. The entire premise of our pact was destroyed and my social life was about to come crumbling down on me like a house of cards.

I cleared my throat. "He really is cute. Mia, you want me to come over and help you study for that big Earth Science test?"

Mia linked her arm in mine. "Yes! It might take us a while. I haven't studied *anything* since the last test you helped me get ready for. You are seriously going to have to be at my house for hours!"

I could feel Maisy trying to catch my eye, but I pretended I didn't notice.

"I'll be there as long as it takes," I said.

MAISY

As usual, Clark was waiting for me at my locker with a book in his hand.

I grabbed the book. "*A Perfect Stranger* by Danielle Steel! You know she's a romance writer, right?"

Clark shrugged. "It was in the box. Told you I wasn't losing this bet."

"My grandma's read every single one of her books." I shook my head and handed the book back to Clark. "Did you know she's written almost two hundred books?"

"Wow! Wonder when she finds time to eat and sleep." Clark shoved the book in the mesh pouch on his backpack, not even caring that the whole world could see he was reading a romance novel from the eighties. "This book's actually not that bad."

I followed Clark out the side door and covered my eyes from the blinding afternoon sun.

As we headed toward the crosswalk, Clark pulled his phone out of his back pocket and read a text. He frowned and shoved the phone back in his pocket.

"What's up?" I asked, stopping at the curb.

He raked his hand through his hair. "Bea just bailed out of the robotics competition."

"What?" I said, even though I shouldn't have been surprised.

"I guess we didn't really need her anyway," Clark said. "We've been meeting on our own without her since that one time at Mia's house anyway."

Bea didn't have to worry about fitting in with the M & Ms because she was already turning into one of them.

"She said she's too busy," Clark continued. "I don't know what she's doing, though. She just bombed the pop quiz in math today, and she screwed up her group project in science with Griffin and Mary Sampson because she never submitted her part of the assignment."

"Um, I think she's distracted because her dad's getting remarried," I said. "Speaking of Bea, she keeps asking me what we've been doing together on Wednesdays and Fridays."

"Did you tell her we've been recruited to a spy ring?" Clark asked.

"You've been reading too many books from the eighties," I said.

The walk signal lit up and Clark and I crossed together, heading for the gleaming marble steps in front of the church.

"She's your best friend, right?" Clark asked, slowing down his steps since I'm so much shorter than him.

"Yeah, but you know what Pastor Bob says all the time. What happens in group—" I started.

"Stays in group," Clark finished. "Obviously. Don't tell people who else is in the group or what they say. But Bea already knows about your mom, and it's no secret about my dad."

"It's not?" I was shocked. "Do Griffin and Marshall know?"

"My dad's the one with the problem. Why should I be embarrassed?" Clark said.

I followed him into church. Even though Clark was so smart, he had a way of making everything seem so simple.

Sometimes group meetings are super relaxed. If no one has anything bad going on, Pastor Bob just lets us talk about whatever we want, like whether hard or soft tacos are better or what show to binge on Netflix.

But this meeting was hard. Really hard. Penelope Ditwater's mom relapsed after being sober for three years and twenty-two days. If her mom who went to meetings every single day and was sober for that long relapsed, how could I be sure Mom wouldn't? Penelope thought she had nothing to worry about. She only came to meetings to give advice to people like Clark and me.

When I got home, Grandma's car was gone, which meant she went to the gym early to watch the end of Addy's practice. The closer it got to the meet, the more nervous Addy was. She liked Grandma to video her so she could watch all the videos later and figure out what she needed to do to make her routine perfect. Of course, Grandma loved to post pictures of Addy doing tricks on Facebook, so it was a win-win for both of them. The only person it wasn't a win for was me, because it meant I was stuck home alone with Mom.

As soon as I got to the front door, I could hear the blaring of the smoke alarm. I opened the door and smoke filled my nose. My heart pounded as I ran to the kitchen ready to drag Mom to safety. I must have gotten home just in time.

Then, I heard laughing. Mom was laughing while the house was clearly burning down. She was in there with Rita Shanklesworth, her old friend, one of the many who had disappeared when Mom was in bad shape.

Rita was standing on a chair waving a magazine at the smoke detector, and Mom was opening the windows.

"What's going on?" I asked. "I was ready to call 9-1-1."

Rita kept waving the magazine. "Nothing to worry about. We just burned some of my cinnamon rolls, that's all."

Mom turned around from the window. Her cheeks were bright pink and she had a big smile on her face. "We were so busy catching up, we forgot all about them."

The fire alarm finally stopped beeping, and Rita hopped off the chair.

I scanned the kitchen for signs that Mom had been up to no good. I don't know what I was looking for. It's not like she would leave her pill bottles out on display.

Mom used a spatula to pop the charred rolls off the baking sheet. "I was hoping we could salvage at least the tops, but these are past saving."

The last time I saw Mrs. Shanklesworth, she had stopped by because she was worried about Mom. She came over with her homemade cinnamon rolls and asked Mom why she had dropped off the face of the earth. When she was heating up the rolls, Mom went in her purse and stole her migraine pills.

It seemed like I was the only person left who hadn't forgiven Mom. Well, I wasn't going to end up like Penelope Ditwater, crying in group because I was so shocked my mom relapsed. I was going to be ready for it to happen, so when it did I could pick up the pieces for Addy and Dad.

CHAPTER SEVENTEEN

BEA

LAST YEAR, I WAS PAINFULLY AWARE OF HOW SILENT MY PHONE was. But over the past few weeks, it had become an extension of my body. There was always a picture to comment on, a Snap to reciprocate, or a group text to respond to. It was easier for me to complete a page full of algebra problems than to think of the funny thing to say in a group text or the right emoji to use. But that phone was my lifeline now.

"Can you put your phone away?" Dad asked. "We finally have some time together, just the two of us."

I shoved it in my backpack, which was at my feet in the front seat of Dad's car. This was typical Dad. Spending every weekend at Peyton and Vivi's soccer games, then giving me a guilt trip for not giving him my undivided attention when he finally had time for me.

"Seems like things are going better for you this year," Dad said. "Monica says you post pictures with your friends all the time."

I swallowed hard. I wished Dad and I had the kind of relationship where I could tell him how hard it was to keep up, how much work went into looking and playing the part. If he were a different dad, I would tell him that I wake up every morning gripped with the fear that it would all go away.

I flashed him a wide smile. "Everything's great."

"That's good," Dad said. "I told you if you stuck it out, you would find your people."

What Dad means is that he didn't want me moving in with him, and he didn't want to pay for private school, so I had no choice but to make it work at Mapleton Middle School.

"You were right, Dad," I said.

"Mom said you're up late all the time doing your homework," Dad said. "She's worried all those honors classes are too much."

Mom must be really worried to have sold me out to Dad. "It's no big deal," I said. "Everyone stays up late doing homework in middle school."

"Monica makes the girls go to bed by nine p.m. sharp on school nights," Dad said. "She says sleep is crucial for kids going through puberty."

I kept my eyes out the window and tried not to gag. No one wants to hear their dad say the word *puberty*.

Dad put on his turn signal and pulled over in front of a random field. He turned off the ignition.

I got a weird feeling in the pit of my stomach. "What's up?"

"So there's something I wanted to talk to you about. Monica thought it would be better if you and me talked about it alone," Dad said.

"I knew it! Monica's pregnant, right? That's why you got the minivan."

Dad started laughing and waving his arms around. "No! Absolutely not! That ship has sailed. I'm not going to be one of those guys with gray hair pushing a baby stroller."

I should've felt relieved, but I knew there was something else coming. A harder punch than a new baby.

I adjusted my face into an encouraging smile. "That's good. I don't want to spend my weekends babysitting for you guys. What is it then?"

"So," Dad started. "Have Peyton or Vivi told you anything about their father?"

That would require them to actually talk to me. I shook my head and tried to keep my face passive. "No."

"He died of a brain aneurysm when Monica was pregnant with Vivi," Dad said.

Guilt and shame washed over me. Now I was the jerk for thinking bad things about them.

"That's awful," I said.

"Vivi never met him and Peyton was so young when he passed away," Dad said. "Monica raised them completely on her own. Until—"

"Until you came along," I finished for him.

Dad nodded.

I knew right then what Dad was going to say, what he was going to ask my permission for. I swallowed hard. "So, you want to adopt them?"

"Yes," Dad said. "But only if it's okay with you. Just think, you'll have real sisters. You've always wanted sisters. Remember you used to beg Mom and me to have a baby?"

I plastered another ear-to-ear grin on my face. "Sisters. That's what I've always wanted."

Dad started the car again. "This is going to be great. I'm doing a little video for Instagram. Kind of like Monica's proposal video, but for the girls."

"Of course you are," I mumbled.

"What was that?" Dad asked.

I looked out the window and said, "Monica will love that."

Dad started the car and hummed while he drove the rest of the way to his new house.

One of the weirdest parts of divorce is having your parents live in two different houses. Mom's house would always be my real home, with the room I had lived in my whole life. I didn't know if I would ever feel like more than a guest in Dad's house.

I saw a curtain swish in the front window, and then Monica threw the front door open. She waved exuberantly the whole time we walked up the path.

As soon as I got to the door, Monica wrapped me in a warm hug. "Hi, Bea!"

"Hi, Monica," I said. "The new house is beautiful."

"Thank you," Monica said. Then she turned to the girls who were sitting on the living room couch. "Girls, say hi to Bea."

Peyton looked up from her laptop and Vivi looked up from her phone. Then they both said, "Hi," at the exact same time. Sharing a last name wasn't going to make me one of them.

"Come see your room!" Monica said.

"Monica worked so hard on it," Dad said.

For a second, I was hopeful they had created a room for me on one of the main floors of the house where everyone else slept. But they brought me down to the basement and stopped in front of the high-end washer and dryer.

I looked around and saw metal racks of clothes and shelves of shoes and accessories. I recognized the tall mirror that Monica used to model clothes for Instagram posts, with the cream rug lined up next to it. It was like getting the behind-the-scenes tour of More Than Mom Jeans. What I didn't see was my room.

I turned around. "I'm confused."

Monica laughed. "Notice anything different from last time we FaceTimed you?"

Dad put his hands on my shoulders and spun me around.

Then I saw it. A wall with an actual door.

Monica waved her arms at the brand-new white door. "That is your new room. I had the contractors put a wall in so you would have your own space."

"Go on," Dad said. "Open the door."

I opened the door, while Monica and Dad stared expectedly at me. It was clear they were waiting for a big reaction.

"Wow!" I said.

"What do you think?" Monica asked. "It was your dad's idea."

"It's very . . . very . . . Harry Potter," I managed to get out.

"Your dad told me how much you love Harry Potter and I just ran with it," Monica said, her face breaking out into a wide smile.

"You really ran with it," I said, running my hand along the stone castle wall façade.

"How cool is that?" Monica said. "I found this wall covering at Target."

"It's great," I said. My cheeks were getting sore from all of the smiling I was doing since Dad picked me up.

Monica had really embraced the Harry Potter theme. She had hung shelves with all of the Harry Potter books. One of the shelves even had a bird cage with a stuffed owl. The bed was covered with a Gryffindor bedspread and there was even a broom hanging over the headboard. It was the perfect bedroom for someone who was obsessed with Harry Potter. But unfortunately, I wasn't and never had been. It was Mom who was into Harry Potter, not me.

MAISY

I woke up to the smell of bacon frying. Addy jumped down from her bed with a loud thump and shouted, "Bacon!" Then she ran down the hall like she hadn't eaten in weeks.

I climbed down from my bed using the ladder like a normal person and headed to the kitchen, hoping Grandma wasn't the one cooking. She usually takes a big skillet, dumps a whole package of bacon in it, and stirs it every now and then until every piece is half burned–half raw.

When I got to the kitchen, Dad was sitting at the table with a steaming cup of coffee and a big smile on his face. "Perfect timing. Your mom's making her famous breakfast sandwiches."

Mom's hair was piled on top of her head in a messy bun and she was wearing her plaid pajamas from three years ago when we were still the kind of family who wore matching pajamas on Christmas morning.

Mom's breakfast sandwiches are legend in our family. Two fried eggs, crispy bacon, drizzles of real maple syrup, and two slices of melted white cheddar sandwiched between two thick pieces of perfectly browned french toast. Back when things were normal, Mom made them for us every Sunday.

Dad held out his sandwich and it looked like something from a cooking video, sliced perfectly down the middle so you could see the layers of melted cheese, bacon, and egg. "Here, take half of mine, while Mom works on the next batch."

"That's okay," I said, ignoring the rumbles in my stomach. "I'm not hungry."

Mom slid her spatula under a fresh sandwich and moved it from the griddle to a plate. "Are you sure, Maisy? I made the bacon extra crispy, the way you like it, and I used your favorite bread from the farmers market."

I shook my head and tried not to inhale the smell of real maple syrup mixed with bacon. "I'm fine. I always eat at Bea's before we walk to school."

Addy took the sandwich and added it to her plate, even though she was already halfway through her own breakfast sandwich.

"Slow down there, Addy, or that sandwich is going to wind up on the mats when you start tumbling," Dad said.

"We're doing homeschool before training today," Addy said, through a mouthful of sandwich.

The only two people who weren't eating were Mom and me. I know it's normal for some moms to skip breakfast, but my mom used to eat breakfast every single day, until she stopped. That was one of the first signs. Of course I was the only person who seemed to notice.

I tried to keep my tone relaxed. "You're not eating, Mom?"

Mom shook her head. "I'm going to yoga this morning with some of my new friends from treatment. Can't do yoga on a full stomach."

Dad munched away on his sandwich like everything was fine. Why was I the only person looking for warning signs?

I narrowed my eyes at Mom. "Isn't there some rule against that?"

"Yoga?" Mom laughed. "I don't think so. I mean, I'm not the best person in the class, but you have to start somewhere, right?"

"I'm talking about hanging out with the other people from treatment. Aren't you supposed to stay away from each other?" I asked.

Dad laughed so hard he spit coffee out. "Your mom's not out on parole."

I didn't understand how he could laugh at a time like this. I almost jumped with relief when Grandma walked in because nothing gets past her. She would notice that Mom was back to her old tricks.

But Grandma poured herself a cup of coffee and sat down like nothing weird was going on.

"Raisa, you want a sandwich?" Mom asked.

"And use up all of my Weight Watchers points in one meal? No, thank you," Grandma said.

Dad started laughing again. "Mom, you don't even do Weight Watchers."

Grandma held up a finger. "But I know all about those points. Bernadette told me how it works and I'm not about to gain twenty pounds from one breakfast sandwich."

I slid my chair back and mumbled, "I need to go get ready for school."

As soon as I got upstairs, I went straight for Mom and Dad's room. I looked under Mom's side of the bed, but there was nothing there except a pair of slippers. I stuck my hand in the slippers but came up empty.

I opened her night table drawer, but the only thing in there was a tube of hand cream, lip balm, and an iPad. I slid my hand between her side of the box spring and mattress, and when I didn't find anything there, I looked under her pillow.

I tiptoed to the door and listened. I could still hear laughing and talking coming from the kitchen, so I moved to Mom's closet. I reached underneath the stacks of folded sweaters but didn't find anything. I reached in her ski jacket pocket.

All of a sudden, the hairs on the back of my neck stood up. I could feel someone standing behind me. I froze, hoping whoever it was would go away.

Mom was standing behind me. "What're you doing, Maisy?"

I turned around slowly, like I was in a horror movie, with my hand still buried in the pocket.

Mom was staring at me, waiting for me to explain why she had just busted me going through her closet. I opened my mouth, but nothing came out.

My stomach instantly knotted up and I felt myself breaking out in a sweat. Of course Dad walked in while I still had one hand deep in the pocket of Mom's coat.

"I thought you were up here getting ready for school and you're going through Mom's things?" Dad asked. "We've been trying to be patient with you, Maisy, but you are making it awfully hard."

I dropped the coat and stood there, desperate to run out of the room, but, unfortunately, Dad was in my way.

Mom reached past me into her closet and grabbed a Poppy Red cardigan that I didn't even know she owned and handed it to me.

"She was looking for this," Mom said. "I told her she could borrow it. It's Maisy's new favorite color. She wears it practically every day."

Mom pushed the sweater into my hands. I had to force my hands open.

"Okay, well you better hurry up," Dad said. He looked at me like he was still suspicious, but not confident enough to make a whole thing out of it. "I can drop you off at school if you want."

"That's okay," I said. "Bea's waiting for me to walk with her."

Of course Mom covered for me with Dad. She owed me for all the times I covered for her. That didn't mean I was going to give up my investigating. I was just going to have to get better at it.

CHAPTER EIGHTEEN

BEA

"YOU DIDN'T RESPOND TO THE GROUP TEXT!" I SAID, AS SOON AS Maisy walked in the back door.

"What group text?" Maisy dumped her backpack on the floor and sat down at the kitchen table.

"The group costume!" I said. "How do you even need to ask?"

Maisy grabbed a banana nut muffin and took a big, crumbly bite. "These girls act like Halloween's the most important thing in the world."

"But you love Halloween," I said, applying a thick layer of lip gloss. "It's your favorite holiday besides Christmas. Remember we used to start planning our costumes over the summer?"

"I hate deciding on the group costume. I don't know why we have to all dress up as the same thing. No one can ever agree on anything and it causes so much drama," Maisy said.

I leaned in closer to the mirror to make sure my concealer was even. Then I swiped highlighter across each cheek. "The top two choices are mermaids or M & Ms."

Maisy leaned her head back and groaned. "Why does Mia insist on M costumes?"

"Mia, Madison, and Chloe voted for M & Ms. Madeline and Meghan want to be mermaids. You and I need to break the tie," I said, "I think we should side with Mia."

Maisy looked down at the rest of her muffin and started picking tiny crumbles off the top.

"You should respond first, and then I'll agree with you," I said.

Maisy stared wordlessly at her pile of muffin crumbs. It felt like she wasn't even in the same room with me.

"Are you even listening? We need to figure this out right now or the costumes won't ship in time. I was thinking we could each wear a different color shirt with a white M on it, tutus that match our shirt, and black leggings."

Maisy's voice was dull and she wasn't even looking at me. "Whatever."

I pointed my makeup brush at her. "When it was my turn to hold up my end of the pact, I put in a lot more effort."

Maisy slid her phone across the table. "Here. Text whatever you want from my phone."

I grabbed her phone and texted.

From: Maisy
To: Mia, Madeline, Meghan, Madison, Chloe, Bea

Let's be M & Ms. So cute! 🍪 🧁 🦄

Then I took my own phone and responded.

From: Bea
To: Maisy, Mia, Madeline, Meghan, Madison, Chloe

Agreed! We all have black leggings. Just need to order the tee shirts and tutus. Here are two Amazon links. 👻 👻 👻 🖤 🖤 🖤

Our phones immediately started pinging with girls claiming their color choices. I put our phones down on the table. "Now that's sorted out, tell me what's going on."

"You want to know where Clark and I have been going?" Maisy asked.

"Yes, if it has something to do with you being in such a bad mood that you don't care about Halloween," I said.

"We're in a group for kids whose parents have substance abuse issues," Maisy said. She looked down at her plate of muffin crumbles. "Like my mom."

I drew in a deep breath. "Clark's mom, too?"

"His dad's an alcoholic," Maisy said. "He caught me crying the morning I found out my mom was coming home. Next thing I knew, we were talking about our parents and he was inviting me to his support group. That's where we've been going every Wednesday and Friday."

Big shock. Maisy was keeping a secret from me.

"Why didn't you tell me? I tell you everything. You've even seen me wearing the ugliest bridesmaid dress on earth."

"It wasn't my secret," Maisy said.

I could feel my cheeks turning red underneath all the foundation. "Don't you trust me?"

Maisy sighed. "Not everything's about you or us, or the pact."

I wanted to say that for me it was. The pact was the only good thing in my life right now. But I took a good look at Maisy, and I noticed the dark circles under her eyes and the downward turn of her mouth.

"Is the group helping?" I asked.

"I thought it was. But one of the girls just told us that her mom relapsed, and it's making me even more anxious about my mom," Maisy said. "If someone's mom could slip up after being sober for years, what about my mom who's been sober for months?"

"That's not going to happen," I said.

"You don't know that. No one does. I just feel like I'm worrying ALL. THE. TIME," Maisy said. "I can't stop looking for signs that she's back to her old tricks."

"I understand how you feel. I start worrying the minute I wake up in the morning," I said, relieved to finally be talking about it.

"Why are you so worried?" Maisy asked.

"I'm still holding my breath waiting for the day Mia boots me from the popular table."

"Are you serious?" Maisy scraped her chair back and jumped up. "Do you really think it's the same thing?"

"Obviously not." I let out a hard breath. "I'm just saying . . ."

Mom burst in the kitchen with wet curls and a weird look on her face. "Have you girls been on Instagram this morning?"

"If it's another viral cat video, we're kind of in the middle—" I started.

Mom swallowed hard. "Um, no, it's not that."

I slung my backpack on one shoulder. "Can you show me later? We have to start walking."

"Sit back down for a second," Mom said. "I'll drive you girls."

I suddenly had a really bad feeling. It got worse when Mom held out her phone and I saw it was open to @morethanmomjeans.

"Did your dad talk to you?" Mom asked.

"What's going on?" Maisy looked from Mom to me and then back to Mom.

I grabbed Mom's phone and hit play, holding it out so Maisy could see.

The camera was zoomed in on the front of Dad's house, which looked like the set of a Halloween movie, with rows of farmers market pumpkins and bales of hay with scarecrows sitting on them.

Monica opened the door and Peyton and Vivi followed behind her. "Wait till you guys see Jim-Dad's latest Halloween decoration."

Vivi clapped her hands together. "Did he get that witch we saw at Home Depot? The one with the cauldron?"

"Better than that." Monica walked to the side of the house, with the girls following close behind.

"Where is it?" Peyton asked.

The camera zoomed in on the black garage door. There were orange lights projected on it, spelling out "CAN I BE YOUR DAD?"

Peyton and Vivi burst into tears and shouted, "Yes!"

Jimmy swooped in the shot and the girls ran over to him and tackled him into a heap of hugs, just as the video ended.

I handed the phone back to Mom.

Maisy reached her hand out to me. "Bea . . ."

I left Maisy's hand there and took two steps toward the door. "Can we go to school now?"

"Bea," Mom started. "Let's talk about this."

I held up my hand. "There's nothing to talk about. Dad already told me."

Mom wrinkled her forehead. "You knew? But why didn't you talk to me about it?"

I turned the doorknob. "We have to go. The M & Ms are waiting at the flagpole for us. We need to make sure everyone ordered their Halloween costumes."

MAISY

"What're you doing?" Addy came bouncing in our room after practice that evening, still running on adrenaline.

I whipped around from my perch standing on my desk chair. It was the only way to see all the way down our street, where Mom was supposedly on one of her evening walks. I was determined to figure out what she was up to when she thought no one was looking. All I had seen so far was her walking, but who knows what she was doing once she turned the corner.

Addy stared at me while I climbed down from the chair.

"I'm keeping track of the moon cycles for science," I said.

"Oh." Addy plopped her gym bag on the floor and kicked off her sneakers.

I wanted to tell her to put her gym stuff on the shelf on her side of the closet, which I had organized for just that purpose, but she looked tired, so I didn't say anything.

Addy spotted my laptop, which was open to the Amazon link for the M & Ms costume. "Cute costume!"

"You don't think it's too obvious?" I asked.

"At least people will know what you guys are." Addy shook her hair down from a tight ponytail.

I realized I had barely seen Addy all week. Grandma had been right about me having the room to myself most of the time. "What's your costume?"

Addy sat on the floor in a full horizontal split and winced as she stretched her body to her right side. "Coach Tracy got us all cat ears, so we don't have to waste time getting in costumes for the gym's Trunk or Treat. She said we have ten minutes, then it's back to practice."

"That sounds awful." I plopped down on our beanbag chair. "I'm not really excited about Halloween, but at least I have a choice."

Addy shrugged. "We don't really care about Halloween with the meet so close. Want to see my floor routine?"

"Yes!"

Addy snuggled up next to me and pulled out her phone. "You're going to love the music. It's a mashup of Ariana Grande's greatest hits."

As Addy tumbled and flipped through the air on her tiny phone screen, I realized I had been so preoccupied with Bea's drama and trying to catch Mom that I hadn't been paying much attention to Addy when we were both actually home at the same time. I gasped as she landed tumbling passes only to leap through the air all over again, while moving with the grace of a dancer.

"This is your best choreo yet, Addy," I said. "You are so talented. It's amazing to see what you can do now."

"Coach Tracy said if I perform it like this at the meet, I'll definitely qualify on floor. I just have to make sure I stick the landing, which is the hardest part." Addy put her phone down on the floor.

"You'll stick the landing," I said, not used to Addy showing a crack in her wall of confidence. "You always do."

Addy got back to stretching in ways that made her body look elastic. "This time it matters more than ever."

"What about the other events?" I asked. "How do you feel about them?"

Addy waved her hand like it was no big deal. "I'm solid on the other three. Floor is the one where I really need to focus."

"Then you better warn Dad not to cheer super loud like he usually does," I said.

Addy laughed, then she whispered, "I had to tell Grandma not to cheer for me at practice."

I buried my head in my hands. "No!"

"It was so embarrassing," Addy said. "It was completely quiet in the gym, and then Grandma started screaming my name."

I laughed. "She is definitely your number one fan. I am so lucky she isn't mine."

Addy laughed. "Agreed."

"What happens if you qualify for level ten at this meet?" I asked.

"Then I try to qualify for Junior Elite by the end of the season," Addy said.

"And then what?" I asked, wanting to hear it out loud.

Addy looked around the room as if checking to make sure no one else was around. She kept her voice low, like she was letting me in on a secret. "I start to try to get on the national team. And then I shoot for the Olympics."

I breathed out hard. "We've been talking about you being in the Olympics since you were two years old and hopped up on the mini bars at the gym and pulled yourself up. But now it's starting to feel real."

Addy shivered. "I know. The closer I get to this, the more it seems like it could actually happen, like I might actually have a shot."

"It's going to happen," I said. "I know it is."

Addy looked at me. "Coach Tracy says I need to be *completely focused* on gymnastics right now. Everything else is a distraction."

"You're getting homeschooled so you can train full-time. You already got rid of all your distractions."

"I did." Addy raised an eyebrow. "But now Mom's back."

I bit my bottom lip. "I thought everything was fine with you and Mom."

"I'm kind of worried about her, too," Addy said.

My whole body instantly tensed up from my shoulders down to my toes. "What? You're the one who keeps saying Mom's fine. How many times did you tell me that I need to trust her?"

Addy blinked really fast like she does when she's trying not to cry. "I *need* to believe Mom's okay. It's the only way I can focus on gymnastics."

I knew I should've been relieved that I wasn't the only one worried, that this wasn't about me being an anxious mess. That maybe I wasn't the only one who hadn't forgiven Mom. But instead, I felt worse. Much worse.

I nodded. "I get it. I'll keep an eye on Mom so you don't have to. You just focus on getting ready for this meet."

"Stop spying on Mom. You're stressing me out," Addy said.

"Someone has to," I said.

Addy shook her head. "Last time, it didn't matter how much we tried to help her. She did what she wanted anyway."

"But, if I—" I started.

"I don't need to be worried about you worrying about Mom, okay?" Addy said.

"Okay," I said.

But I knew there was no way that was going to happen. I would just have to get better at hiding it.

⇒⋯ CHAPTER NINETEEN ⋯⇐

BEA

I PULLED ON MY YELLOW TUTU AND TUCKED IN MY YELLOW T-SHIRT
so the white M was centered. Of course, I got stuck being the yellow
M & M because I let everyone else pick their colors first. I guess I was
destined to wear colors I hated just to stay visible.

I walked into the kitchen and found Mom and Mr. Pembrook
dressed as Professor McGonagall and Dumbledore.

My stomach dropped when I imagined them walking around
town holding hands.

"I thought you guys were staying home tonight," I said.

"Someone has to pass the candy out," Mom said.

"We have our whole night planned," Mr. Pembrook said through
his gray painted beard. He was taping a sign to a teal plastic pumpkin
that said GLUTEN, DAIRY, AND PEANUT FREE.

"We're watching Harry Potter movies, eating Veggie Palace takeout, and handing candy out." Mom clapped her hands together. "Doesn't that sound like the perfect night?"

"Um, for you guys, yes, that sounds like the perfect night," I said. I was glad we were trick-or-treating in Mia's neighborhood.

Maisy walked in the back door wearing her green M & M costume, and I instantly felt jealous because she looked so much better than I did.

"You guys look so cute!" Mom's face broke into a smile. "This is just like the old days. Bea, stand next to Maisy. We need a picture."

"Wait," Maisy said. "Let me get a picture of you guys first so you can post it on Facebook. #couplegoals."

Mom scooted in closer to Mr. Pembrook, her witch hat knocking into his wizard hat, while Maisy took their picture. I don't know whose smile was bigger, Mom's or Mr. Pembrook's. I could see the writing on the wall. One month after Monica started posting with Dad on social media, she had moved in with him. The last thing I needed was my supposed best friend encouraging Mom and Mr. Pembrook.

Maisy handed the phone back to Mom. "I took a lot."

Mom held out her phone, slid her finger across the screen and showed me. "What about this one?"

I shrugged. "They all look the same to me."

Maisy gave Mom an awkward look. "You guys look great in all of them."

Mom looked up from her phone. "What's your plan for the night?"

"Trick-or-treating in Mia's development," I said.

Maisy pulled a Twizzler from the teal pumpkin and ripped the wrapper off with her teeth. "They give out full-sized candy bars."

"Just be careful," Mr. Pembrook said. "There's something about costumes that make ordinarily good kids get up to no good."

Mom laughed. "Maisy and Bea never get in trouble on Halloween."

Mr. Pembrook looked at me. "Even good kids make mistakes."

Mom waved her hands at him. "Not these girls."

"We have to go," I said, nudging Maisy toward the door.

Mom grabbed a bag of Skittles from the pumpkin. "I'll pick you up in front of Mia's at nine thirty."

"No one's going home that early," I said. "It's Halloween!"

"It's a school night," Mom said.

Maisy adjusted her tutu. "I have to be home by then anyway."

"Don't want to be too tired for math tomorrow," Mr. Pembrook said.

"Definitely need to be awake for my fave class." Maisy reached out and gave him a fist bump.

I grabbed Maisy's hand. "Come on, Maisy. Let's go."

When we got to Mia's, the other M & Ms were waiting for us and it hit me how far I had come from last year when I was the one staying home with Mom to hand out candy. I remember looking out the window and watching the groups of kids trick-or-treating. All I wanted was to be part of one of those groups who were wearing a theme costume. And now here I was standing in Mia's foyer while her mom took pictures of us in our matching tutus.

"Make sure you girls hit up Spruce Lane first before all the full-sized candy bars are gone," Mia's mom said. Her costume had about a quarter of the fabric of Mom's wizard cloak. She was dressed as a black cat in black leather moto leggings, a black crop top, and tiny kitten ears and a kitten tail. Mia's dad honked from the car.

"Gotta go, girls," she said, blowing kisses at all of us on her way out the door. "Have fun."

"You guys ready?" Meghan asked. "I heard the Murphys are giving out king-sized Snickers."

Chloe looked stricken. She stared at Madison and seemed to be talking to her with her eyes.

"Guys!" Madison waved her hands around to make sure everyone was paying attention. "Chloe's allergic to peanuts."

"O-k-a-y." Meghan stretched the word out in a fake serious tone. "We won't feed her any peanut candy."

Chloe blinked several times. "Yeah, but I have an airborne peanut allergy."

Madison sounded more serious than I had ever heard her before. "That means we can't eat peanuts around her or she could, like, die."

"I know how to use an EpiPen," Madeline said. "My cousin's allergic to peanuts, too."

"Sorry about your cousin," Chloe said. "Um, I think I need to avoid using the EpiPen."

"So what does this mean?" Mia threw her hands up. "Are you telling us we can't trick-or-treat?"

"We could go to the houses with the teal pumpkins," Madeline said. "They have all allergy-safe treats."

"Everyone knows the stuff at the teal pumpkin houses sucks. Half of them don't even give out candy. I mean, what are we going to do with stickers and plastic spiders?" Mia said.

"Some of the teal pumpkins have candy in them," I said, thinking about the Skittles, Sour Patch Kids, and Twizzlers Mr. Pembrook had piled in our teal pumpkin.

Mia rolled her eyes. "Candy no one wants."

Chloe's face fell. "It's okay. I'll just go home."

"You're not leaving." Madison grabbed her arm. "Right, guys?"

I pretended to be fascinated with the intricate floorboards in Mia's foyer. It was so quiet I could hear the ticking from the fancy grandfather clock in the foyer. Each second felt like an hour.

Maisy was the first person to speak up. "What if we trick-or-treat at all the houses, but no one eats anything with peanuts while Chloe's around? We can all just save the unsafe candy for later. Chloe, would that work?"

"Yes!" Chloe's face flooded with relief. "Can you guys do that?"

Madeline jumped right in. "Yes!" Then she stared at the other girls. "We can do that. Right?"

Mia sighed as if someone was asking her to give up candy for the rest of her life. "Fine. Let's go before there isn't any candy left."

The other girls followed behind her, with dramatic sighs.

"You're lucky we're such good friends," Madeline said to Chloe on the way out the door.

Maisy grabbed my arm and hissed at me, "What's wrong with you?"

I shook my head. "What?"

"If one of the Sunflower girls had a peanut allergy, you'd have their back," Maisy said.

"It's not like I was going to eat peanuts around her. I just didn't need to be the one to start drama with everyone else," I said.

"Start drama? By suggesting that we don't eat something around someone who's deathly allergic to it?" Maisy said.

"You know what I mean," I said.

"Congratulations. You finally got what you wanted. You've turned into an M & M," Maisy said.

MAISY

I'm not really a fan of trick-or-treating. It's always cold, but putting on a jacket ruins your costume. I like candy as much as the next person, but there's only so much candy you can eat before you start feeling sick. Back in the days when it was just Bea and me, we trick-or-treated just long enough to get the right amount of candy, then we would go home and snuggle on the couch and watch *Hocus Pocus*. The morning after Halloween, Heather always makes her famous "trick-or-treat pancakes." She chops up mini chocolate bars from Bea's candy stash and mixes them in her pancake batter. I wished we could just go back to our old traditions before either one of us was an M & M.

Now I was stuck trailing along after the M & Ms in search of all the full-sized candy bars in Mapleton when I should really be keeping an eye on Mom. She hadn't finished her dinner last night, even though we had everyone's favorite meal, Spaghetti à la Dad. She told us she was still full because they ordered pizza at her program for lunch, but how do you believe someone who just spent the past two years lying about *everything*? Now that I knew Addy was just as concerned as me, it made me stop second-guessing my suspicions. There was concrete evidence out there about what Mom was really up to. I just needed to find it.

I sat on the edge of the sidewalk while the M & Ms were emptying out a candy bowl someone had left on their porch with a sign that said TAKE ONE, PLEASE.

"Hey, Maisy."

I looked up.

Clark towered over me wearing a baseball uniform with rye bread glued all over it. He was also wearing a catcher's mask and a baseball glove.

I stood up to get a closer look at his costume. "What are you supposed to be?"

He pointed to his catcher's mask. "Catcher in the . . ." He pointed to the bread that was stuck to his uniform. "Rye."

I laughed really hard for the first time all night. "That's perfect and totally you."

I watched as the M & Ms ran up to the next porch.

Clark pushed up his catcher's mask, squinted hard, and pretended to sound confused. "Let me guess. You guys are M & Ms?"

"There's no stumping you," I said. "No wonder you got into all those honors classes."

"We missed you at the last meeting," Clark said. "Pastor Bob made these brownie cookie dough combo things that were so good."

I looked down at the ground. "I just . . . That last meeting was so hard."

"I get it. It made me suspicious of everything my dad was doing," Clark said.

I felt the tight air that was trapped in my chest loosen up. "OMG! You too?"

"Come back," Clark said. "It's not as much fun without you. You're the only other person who can eat as many cookies as me."

I sighed. "Meet me at my locker tomorrow."

Clark smiled. "K. Gotta go find Griffin and Marshall."

He ran off yelling, "Has anyone seen Ant Man or Iron Man?"

I ran to catch up with the M & Ms, who were now four houses down. By the time I got to them, they were crowding around Terrance and his best friend, Mark. We had seen them throughout the night ringing doorbells and asking for candy even though they weren't wearing costumes. Terrance may be the new Glow Up, but my vote was still with Clark.

I knew something was up as soon as I got over to them because Bea wouldn't make eye contact with me. The little hairs on my arms stood up and I heard a ringing in my ears. I had a really bad feeling about hanging out with them.

"Most of the houses are out of candy by now," Terrance said.

Mark popped a blue Blow Pop out of his mouth and said, "Everyone ran out of full-sized bars hours ago." He was wearing a black hoodie with white skeleton bones on it, but it didn't come across as Halloweenish because he wore it to school all the time.

Mia nodded. "My parents are at a party anyway. They won't know the difference if we're trick-or-treating or doing other things."

I felt a weird pull in my stomach. I didn't want to know what those other things were.

"As long as we're all at Mia's in time for pickup, none of our parents will know the difference," Madeline said.

I tried to catch Bea's eye, but she didn't turn toward me.

"I'm in," Mia said. Which, of course, meant we were all in.

Terrance gave her a fist bump and then motioned for us to follow him and Mark across the street to the deserted Green Grocer parking lot.

The boys opened up their pillowcases and we all leaned over to look inside. I expected to see a stash of candy, but there were cans of shaving cream, cartons of eggs, and rolls of toilet paper in each of their bags.

Mia clapped her hands together. "This is going to be so much fun! I've always wanted to do Mischief Night."

"We're a day late for that," I said. "Mischief Night was last night."

"Exactly," Terrance said. "No one will expect it tonight."

"My dad's Jeep got egged last year and it destroyed the paint. He had to pay to get the whole car repainted. It was *really* expensive," I said.

"Isn't your dad a doctor?" Terrance said. "I'm sure he can swing a new paint job."

"Ever heard of something called insurance?" Mark piped in.

"We have a high deductible. And just because someone can afford something doesn't mean they should have to pay for it," I said.

"We won't egg anyone's car that we know," Madeline said.

"That doesn't make it right," I said.

Mark handed me a roll of toilet paper. "You can stick to this then."

I didn't take the toilet paper. Instead, I stared him down.

Madison grabbed the roll of toilet paper from Mark and grabbed another one from his bag for Chloe. "We're in."

I looked around at the other girls. "Are you guys all seriously gonna do this?"

"Trick-or-treating was getting so boring," Meghan said.

"And stressful with the whole peanut allergy thing," Madeline said. "No offense, Chloe, but it's super triggering to have to worry about a peanut allergy, since my cousin almost died from it."

Chloe nodded. "I totally get it."

"You guys coming or not?" Terrance said.

I hoisted my haul of candy on my shoulder and took a step back. "I'm going home."

Mia held up her hand. "Can you guys give us one sec?"

Terrance and Mark looked at each other and walked to the other side of the parking lot.

Mia lashed out as soon as they were out of earshot. "What's your problem, Maisy?"

"I have a problem just because I don't want to break the law?" I said.

"You've been in your own little world lately," Meghan said. "You barely come to Mia's house anymore and now all of a sudden you're into doing your own thing."

"It's called thinking for myself. You guys should try it some-time," I said.

"The whole point of being in a group is not having to think for yourself," Madison said.

"I'm going," I said. "You coming, Bea?"

Bea looked down at the ground.

"I guess I have my answer." I walked out of the parking lot and headed home.

CHAPTER TWENTY

BEA

MADELINE LOOKED UP FROM THE PILE OF CANDY SHE WAS SORT-ing. "OMG! Did you see the look on Mrs. Peterson's face when she saw her front yard?"

"It's going to take her forever to clean up all that toilet paper," Meghan said, while she swapped out two mini Twixes for two of Madison's full-sized Milky Ways.

I checked my phone for what felt like the hundredth time. Maisy still hadn't texted. I grabbed my pillowcase full of candy and stood up. "See you guys later. I'm going outside to wait for my mom."

Mia jumped up and wrapped me in a big hug. "Tonight was epic! Byeee!"

Dealing with Mia was easier than being around Maisy right now. It was less complicated with Mia. All I had to do was whatever she wanted and she was happy. Lately, I never knew what Maisy was thinking. I never knew when she was going to come down hard on me.

When I got outside, I pulled out a king-sized Milky Way and ripped open the wrapper with my teeth. The last thing I wanted to do was eat more candy, but kids who didn't get into trouble on Halloween eat their candy until their mom tells them not to.

Mr. Pembrook's Prius pulled up to the curb. I looked back at Mia's windows to make sure the M & Ms weren't looking, then I opened the car door. I climbed into the back seat and hunched down a bit so no one would see me when Mr. Pembrook started driving.

"Where's Mom?"

"She kept falling asleep with her hand in the bowl of popcorn while we watched TV, so I told her I would come get you," Mr. Pembrook said.

I took a bite of my Milky Way. "Halloween always wipes Mom out."

"We were the hottest house on the block. I had to go out and buy more candy," he said. "It's terrible how many kids have food allergies these days. It's an epidemic."

The Milky Way caught in my throat. I folded the wrapper over and put the rest of the bar in my pillowcase.

"Got any Jolly Ranchers?" Mr. Pembrook asked.

I reached in my pillowcase and grabbed out a handful of Jolly Ranchers and handed them to him.

"Thanks." Mr. Pembrook dumped the candy in his cup holder. He unwrapped a piece and popped it in his mouth while we sat at a red light.

"Your pillowcase is overflowing. Looks like you hit quite a few houses," Mr. Pembrook said, with the Jolly Rancher clacking against his teeth.

I felt a little queasy when I thought about how many porches we had sprayed with shaving cream and hit with eggs. We had gone through Terrance's Costco-sized case of toilet paper and draped trees and bushes with layer upon layer of thin paper. The worst, though, was when the boys started smashing jack-o'-lanterns. It made me think of when I was in first grade and Mom and I walked out of the house the morning after Halloween and found our little pumpkin family smashed into pulpy bits on the sidewalk. That was the last Halloween before Dad left, and his pumpkin face had been smeared all over the sidewalk.

"What happened to Maisy?" he asked. "Your mom said I was supposed to drive her home, too."

I should've made up a lie, but I was too tired. Halloween can be exhausting.

"We got in a fight," I said.

Mr. Pembrook nodded. "There's something about Halloween that stirs up drama. I have a theory about it."

"What's the theory?" I asked, hoping he would say something that would make me feel like less of a jerk.

"You take a bunch of kids who don't normally hang out on the streets when it's dark, let them run around town dressed up like alternate personalities, and get them hopped up on candy. Perfect formula for drama," he said.

"That actually makes a lot of sense," I said.

Maybe tonight wasn't completely my fault.

"Do you have Reese's Peanut Butter Cups for—" Mr. Pembrook asked.

"Mom? Yeah. I save them for her every year," I said. "I got a stash of full-sized ones for her."

Mr. Pembrook smiled at me through the rearview mirror and his teeth were Jolly Rancher pink. "Great. That will make her happy."

"Thanks for coming to get me," I said. "I'm not used to having someone besides Mom around to pick me up."

I also wasn't used to having someone else around who looked out for Mom. It wasn't just the Halloween candy. He was always doing nice things for her: he starts her car and runs the heat on cold mornings and he lets her eat all the corner pieces when he makes black bean brownies.

"I'm not used to having anyone else besides me to worry about. It's really nice," Mr. Pembrook said.

The nicer Mr. Pembrook was, the more I felt like a fraud. If he only knew he was driving home a vandal.

Mr. Pembrook pulled into the driveway and turned the car off. "I get that you're still getting used to me dating your mom. *I'm* still getting used to me dating your mom. Thanks for putting up with me being around so much."

I looked down at my bag full of candy so I didn't have to make awkward eye contact with Mr. Pembrook. "It's nice to see Mom happy."

He turned around in his seat and reached out his hand. "Give me your phone."

"Okay," I said, handing it to him, nervous he was going to look through my pictures and discover evidence of our mischief making.

Mr. Pembrook moved his finger over the screen. "I added my number to your contacts. That way you can call me if you ever need a ride or whatever."

I giggled awkwardly. "Um, thanks. I should be all set, though."

Mr. Pembrook set his mouth in a straight line. "I don't know what it's like to be a parent, but I do remember what it's like to be in middle school. That means I know how quickly things can escalate. One minute everything's fine, and next thing you know, you end up in a really bad situation."

I got busy smoothing out my T-shirt and adjusting my tutu.

"You can always call me and I'll come pick you up wherever you are." Mr. Pembrook looked me right in the eye. "No questions asked."

If only he knew his offer was coming a few hours too late.

"Thanks," I said.

I hoisted my candy bag over my shoulder and headed to the front door.

"Bea, wait," Mr. Pembrook said.

I turned around. "What?"

He held out a half-used-up roll of toilet paper. "You dropped this."

MAISY

The next morning, I was brushing my teeth when Addy barged in the bathroom wearing a leotard with warm-up pants. "You and Bea are in a fight?"

My whole body buzzed as I spit out the glob of foamy toothpaste. "How do you know?"

Addy held up her phone, which was open to Bea's latest Instagram post. "She just posted," she said.

The M & M s were sitting around Bea's kitchen table, their plates piled high with Heather's famous "trick-or-treat pancakes." She had swapped out her usual chopped-up chocolate bars for Twizzlers, Swedish Fish, and Sour Patch Kids.

All of a sudden, Bea has a conscience about Chloe's peanut allergy.

"What happened?" Addy asked, while she pulled on a thick gray hoodie.

"Halloween drama," I said, handing the phone back to Addy. I had seen enough.

Addy shook her head. "Whatever you did, you should say sorry."

I pulled a hairbrush through my tangled hair. "How do you know it's my fault? She's the one hanging out with all of *my* friends!"

"You can be a little judgy, that's all," Addy said.

"You're my sister. You're supposed to be on my side," I said.

Addy flipped her ponytail over her shoulder. "I'm just trying to help."

I sat down on my bed. I knew I shouldn't do it, but I couldn't help myself. I opened up Bea's Instagram stories. The first picture was the one Heather took of us in the kitchen. We stood side by side wearing our M & M costumes with big smiles on our faces. I wanted to shake the girls in the picture and say, "Just stay home." The next picture was the group picture of all of us in our costumes at Mia's house. An outsider looking in would think we were all the best of friends, with no drama. That was the last appearance I made in her story.

When I got to school, I was glad I didn't have any morning classes with Bea. The other M & Ms froze me out, except Chloe, who gave me a sympathetic smile when no one was looking. Mia and Meghan didn't say one word to me in math, and in PE Madison and Madeline looked right through me. I had switched places with Bea. Now that I knew what it felt like to be invisible, I started to feel bad. But hadn't I done enough to make it up to her?

When the lunch bell rang, I headed straight to the library. I found Griffin, Marshall, and Clark at a table in the back working on their drone over boxed cafeteria lunches and piles of Halloween candy.

"I think this is where the compartment should go," Griffin said, pointing his finger at the bottom of the drone.

"I think it's more aerodynamic to put it here," Marshall argued.

I clapped my hands together. "OMG! Are you guys really putting in a sunblock dispenser?"

Marshall pushed up his glasses higher on his nose. "Of course. That was a really smart idea."

"Thanks," I said, feeling a smile creep back on my face for the first time since Halloween. I wasn't used to being called smart.

"Got any other ideas?" Griffin asked through a mouthful of turkey sandwich.

Marshall cut in. "We heard these kids from Sugar Lake Middle School are making a robot that can help make your bed. That's going to be tough to beat."

"Did you already connect it to Spotify?" I asked.

"Yeah," Clark said. "That was genius."

"We need one more thing, though." Marshall held out a bag of Doritos to me.

I reached in and grabbed a Dorito. "What if you add some kind of timer to the sunblock dispenser?"

Clark rested his chin in his hand like he was thinking it through. "What would the timer be for?"

I grabbed another couple of Doritos. "There are two reasons people get sunburned. The first one is that they're too lazy to get up to put the sunblock on. You already fixed that. The second reason is that they lose track of the time and forget when they need to reapply."

Griffin, Clark, and Marshall stared at me.

"I know it's kind of a dumb idea," I said. "I just thought it might give you guys more points."

"No, it's actually a perfect idea. Adding in the time element will push our score to the next level," Marshall said.

He was so excited, I didn't have the heart to tell him that he had bread stuck in his braces.

Clark pulled out a chair. "Come sit with us. You can help."

"Um, actually, I need your help with something," I said. "But it's kind of, you know, personal."

Griffin waved at Clark. "Go ahead. We got this."

Marshall and Griffin leaned over the drone and got right back to work.

Clark took out a big set of keys and jangled them. "Let's go to the chem lab."

"Perfect," I said.

I followed Clark out of the library while Griffin and Marshall started back in on their dispenser debate.

I whipped out my cell phone as soon as we got to the chem lab. "I need help with the Find My Friends app. I keep looking for my mom's icon but can't see it. I must be doing something wrong."

"You didn't . . ." started Clark.

"It's the only way to be sure my mom's really spending her days at treatment. My dad's at work all day. He has no idea what she's really up to," I said.

Clark shook his head. "You don't want to do this."

I piled my hair on top of my head in a messy topknot. "Pastor Bob's always talking about closure. Maybe if I see she's really at treatment every day, I can finally have some closure."

"This isn't a good idea, Maisy," Clark said.

"You heard Griffin and Marshall. They said I'm a genius and I come up with really good ideas."

Clark smirked. "Don't let it go to your head or anything."

"Seriously," I said. "This morning my sister called me judgy. I need to know if I'm really judgy or if I'm actually right about my mom."

"Why don't you talk about this in group today?" Clark suggested.

I crossed my arms. "What do you think's gonna help me more? Talking about how I think my mom's up to no good or finding out for sure?"

"Fine, but I'm going on the record here. This is a really bad idea," Clark said.

"Okay, okay." I nodded slowly. "I get it. It's a bad idea. Now can you show me how to work this?"

Clark swiped his finger across the screen a few times and pointed to an icon. "Your mom's here."

"How did you find her? I looked *everywhere* in Mapleton for her," I said.

Clark chewed on his thumbnail. "Um, where is she *supposed* to be?"

"At Five Rivers Health Center, which is right next to Maple Grove Shopping Center," I said.

Clark zoomed in closer. "Are you sure she's supposed to be there now? Does she get a lunch break or something?"

"Where is she?" I asked, standing on my tiptoes to see the phone.

Clark held the phone higher, so it was out of my reach. "Maisy, I told you we shouldn't do this."

I jumped up and grabbed the phone. "I got a C on my map skills quiz. I don't know how to read this. Where is she?"

Clark looked at me with sorry eyes. "She's not in Mapleton. That's why you couldn't find her."

The air whooshed out of my mouth. "What?"

"It looks like she's in the Sugar Creek Shopping Center," Clark said. "But that doesn't mean . . ."

I moved my fingers on the screen until the map became easier to read. There was my mom's icon right in the middle of the shopping center. I Googled *What stores are in the Sugar Creek Shopping Center?*

"Good idea," Clark said. "She's probably just clothes shopping on her lunch break or something. My mom drives all over the place for the perfect outfit."

I looked up from my phone. "Or she's at CVS."

Clark furrowed his brow. "Why would she be—"

"The last time she stole my dad's prescription pad, she went to a pharmacy in another town. A pharmacy where no one would know her or my dad."

→·· CHAPTER TWENTY-ONE ··←

BEA

I WALKED OUT OF THE CAFETERIA WITH THE M & MS AND SCANNED THE crowded hallway for Maisy. I still couldn't believe she hadn't shown up for Mom's annual post-Halloween pancakes. It's our tradition. I figured she'd cool off and everything could go back to normal, but not only did she ditch us for breakfast, she was a no-show for lunch, too.

"Did you see the Thompson house this morning?" Meghan asked. "My dad drove past on our way to school and he said Mrs. Thompson was going to have to hire someone to get all that toilet paper out of her trees."

"I feel kind of bad," Madison said.

"Um, what about the time you babysat the twins for eight hours and she paid you twenty dollars?" Meghan said. "Her kids are the biggest brats ever and she didn't even pay you minimum wage."

"I forgot all about that! She totally deserved it," Madison said.

But I thought of the time Mom's car wouldn't start and Mr. Thompson jump-started it for her while Mrs. Thompson drove me to school so I wouldn't be late.

As we walked past the chem lab, Mia stopped short and Madison and Chloe slammed into her.

"No way," Meghan said, as she leaned over Mia to look in the lab window.

"This explains why Maisy's been acting so weird lately," Madeline said.

I pushed my way through the girls and stuck my head between Madison's and Chloe's.

At least now I knew where Maisy was. Her face was pressed into Clark's chest and his arms were wrapped around her.

"Whoa." Mia whipped around to face me. "Bea, did you know about this?"

I felt like I had been punched in the gut. No matter how many times I begged Maisy to open up to me, she was still keeping secrets. She was still choosing someone else over me.

I shook my head because I couldn't make words come out of my mouth.

"Who knew Maisy would be the first one to choose a guy over us?" Madeline said.

Me. I should've known. I should've known because last year she chose the M & Ms over me. Clark was just the next new, cooler thing.

"And she waits until after we decide he's not Glow Up material?" Meghan said.

"Seriously, now that Terrance is the new Glow Up, Clark is back to what he's always been, a nerd who hangs out with other nerds," Mia said. "She's going to ruin her reputation and bring us down with her."

My heart sank. If Maisy lost her spot in the M & Ms, what did that mean for me? I didn't have strong enough footing yet to be guaranteed a spot with them. I replayed those thoughts in my head and realized that as mad as I was at Maisy, I also needed to protect her.

"Guys, it's not what it looks like," I whispered, as I took a few steps away from the window, hoping they would follow me.

"Oh, so Maisy's not ditching us for Clark?" Meghan said, her arms folded and her eyes narrowed.

"When was the last time she came over to hang out with us after school?" Madeline added.

Madison looked at Chloe. "Chloe and I saw her and Clark walking home from school together last week."

"They're obviously dating," Meghan said. "If we were really her best friends, she would tell us."

"So we're obviously not her best friends," Madison jumped in.

"They're not dating," I said, in as confident a tone as I could muster. "I would know."

Mia tilted her head. "Would you, though?"

Her words hit me because I knew she was right. Maisy has a pretty solid track record of keeping things from me.

"This is going to ruin us," Madeline said. "If word gets out that Maisy's dating the head of the nerd herd, none of the normal guys will want to date any of us."

The words fell from my mouth before I could even think. "They're not dating. They're in a group together for children of addicts."

Mia started blinking rapidly. "What?"

"Maisy's mom is addicted to prescription pills and Clark's dad is an alcoholic," I said.

Madison scrunched up her face. "Maisy's mom is a drug addict? Like the people we see on Main Street begging for money?"

Madeline let out a long sigh. "You don't have to be homeless to have a drug problem, Madison."

I tried to get the conversation back on track. "Maisy hasn't been ditching us on purpose. She's been going to meetings," I said. "With Clark, for kids like them."

Maisy didn't know it, but we had changed places. I was back to being the one keeping her in the group, just like I did at Camp Amelia.

"And she didn't tell us?" Madeline said. "I thought we were supposed to be her friends."

"Her best friends," Madison added.

"Yeah," Mia chimed in. "Aren't you supposed to tell your best friends everything?"

I swallowed hard. Maybe Mia was right. If Maisy really was my best friend, she should be confiding in me, not Clark. Once again, Maisy was pulling away from me and leaning on someone else.

MAISY

Clark held open the church door, and the bright afternoon sun shone in our faces as we walked outside. I shivered as the wind whipped through the trees that lined the church lawn.

"It got a lot colder since the meeting started," I said.

Clark unzipped his hoodie and handed it to me. "You might have to roll the sleeves up a few times, but at least it will keep you warm."

"Aren't you going to be cold?" I asked.

"I'll be fine." Clark pressed the sweatshirt into my hands. "You take it."

I pulled on the sweatshirt and it hung down to my knees. It felt warm and cozy and smelled just like Clark, a mix of simple soap and high-quality shampoo.

"Thanks," I said, rolling the sleeves up.

"You should've spoken at the meeting today," Clark said. "We spent half the time talking about whether the varsity football team has a shot at playoffs when you actually had something real to talk about."

"It feels too weird," I said. "You guys have all been in group together for years. You can just jump right into a story and everyone knows all the important history. I feel like it's too much work. There's too much to explain."

"You have to start somewhere," Clark said. "No one is ever going to know your history if you don't start telling them part of your story."

"I don't know how to talk about my mom without sounding pissed. No one else ever seems mad." I pulled the hood of Clark's sweatshirt on top of my hair and then shoved my hands in the pockets.

"You just started coming to group, and, like you said, most of these kids have been coming for years. You just missed the part when they were where you are now," Clark said.

"Maybe there's something wrong with me because I don't think I'm ever going to be like those other kids in group," I said. "I can't imagine not being mad anymore."

He smiled at me in a sad way. "I felt the exact same way when I first started going to meetings."

"Come on, I'll race you to the corner of my street." I was done with talking, so I sprinted ahead.

"Wow! You're really fast," Clark said, trying to catch his breath when he got to the corner seconds after me.

"Thanks." I put both hands on the bottom of the hoodie, ready to pull it off and give it back to Clark.

But Clark reached out and put one of his hands over mine. "You don't have to give it back."

I felt a little zing on the top of my hand where his hand was. But then he moved his hand and the feeling went away.

"Are you sure? I'm home now," I said.

Clark turned toward the direction of his street. "You never know when you might need it again."

I watched as he turned down the street. I rubbed the spot where he had touched my hand and felt that little zing again.

When I got near my house, I noticed right away that Mom's car wasn't in the driveway, which meant I had a little time to search the one place I hadn't yet. I ran upstairs and straight to her craft room. It felt weird being in that room, because it looked like the old Mom's. Everything was organized and neat, bolts of fabric shelved in color order, tiny drawers filled with buttons, thread, and ribbons. There was a place for everything, and everything fit in exactly the right place.

Hanging up on the back of the door was my Dorothy costume from *The Wizard of Oz*. I pulled the blue-and-white checked dress down and held it close to me. I sank to the floor with the dress in my arms. That was the last costume Mom made. She hurt her Achilles tendon a few weeks after the show, and that's when the doctor prescribed her pain meds and things fell apart.

I heard the front door swing open and my heart started beating out of my chest. I jumped up and hung the dress back up on the door. No one would ever know I had been in there.

"Maisy?" Dad called up the stairs.

I was so glad he was home before Mom. All I had to do was run down the stairs and show him the screenshot of Mom hanging out in Sugar Creek while she was supposedly at treatment. Then he would have to realize I had been right all along.

"Coming!" I yelled, running downstairs with my phone in my hand.

"Careful on those stairs!" Dad called. "I can't tell you how many broken bones I see from people falling."

"Dad, I really need to . . ." I started.

I froze on the bottom step. "Mom? What're you doing here?"

Dad was walking in front of Mom, with a stack of pizza boxes in his hand. "Special delivery," he said. "I brought home pizza and your mom."

"Dad got enough pizza for ten people!" Mom said, as if it was any ordinary day, as if she didn't have anything to feel guilty about.

"Addy counts as four people," Dad said. "Especially after practice."

Mom laughed. "So true."

I followed them into the dining room, trying to calm my heart rate without making it obvious.

Dad put the pizza boxes down on the dining room table. "What were you about to tell me?"

I looked down at the rug. "Nothing."

Mom opened up a big white paper bag and started pulling out napkins, utensils, and paper plates.

"Come sit down, Maisy, while the pizza's still hot," Dad said.

I slid into my usual seat, but there was nothing ordinary about this dinner. This was the moment Dad was going to have to face the truth.

Mom grabbed a slice right from the box and took a bite without even putting it on a plate first. "I'm starving!" she said through a mouthful of pepperoni pizza.

"I bet you are," I mumbled.

"What was that, Maisy?" Mom said.

Dad put a paper plate in front of me, then he loaded it up with one piece of white pizza and a lasagna slice. "We got your favorites, Maisy."

I smiled weakly at him. "Thanks."

I turned to Mom. "How was your program today, Mom?"

From the corner of my eye, I could see Dad looking happy that I was actually talking to Mom, and for a split second I felt guilty.

"Great. I'm getting to know the people in my group," Mom said.

"What's the program like? Do you sit in a room talking all day?" I asked.

This was the moment I had been waiting for. I was going to catch her in a lie, then show Dad my screenshot of her hanging out in Sugar Creek. Then she could go back to rehab and stay there forever, for all I cared.

Mom looked me in the eyes and held my gaze. I don't know how, but she knew.

"We went on a field trip today," she said.

I sat back in my chair. Of course Mom had a perfectly reasonable excuse. She was always one step ahead of me.

"You didn't tell me that," Dad said, while he wiped the pizza grease off his chin. "Where did you go?"

"We went to one of those escape rooms," Mom said. "You know that new place in Sugar Creek, where you get locked in a room and have to figure out clues to get out?"

"Jenny and Carlos, our surgery nurses, are obsessed with that place. They suggested we plan a staff day there for team building," Dad said.

"It would be perfect for that. We've been working on techniques for when we feel frustrated, and this was the perfect place to use them," Mom said.

"Were the counselors with you guys the whole time?" I asked.

Mom laughed. "Uh, yeah, they were stuck with us until we figured out how to get out of that locked room. I actually felt kind of bad for them, but then I remembered they were getting paid an awful lot to be stuck in that room with us."

"Then what did you guys do?" I asked. "After the escape room?"

Dad cut me off, waving his slice of pepperoni pizza at me. "Who cares what they did after? I want to hear about the room. Was it the pirate ship one?"

I tuned everyone out while Mom described the murder mystery room she was trapped in. I was the one who felt trapped, in a family where I was the only person who could see what was really going on.

CHAPTER TWENTY-TWO

BEA

"WHAT'RE YOU STILL DOING HERE?" MOM ASKED, AS SHE WALKED
into the kitchen. She immediately slipped off her house-showing
heels and shook her curls loose from the topknot. "I thought you had
plans with your dad this afternoon."

"He rescheduled," I said, busying myself with putting on lip gloss
in the mirror so she couldn't see my face.

"What? You guys had this special day planned for weeks. Just the
two of you," Mom said. "Your last day together before the wedding."

I put away the lip gloss and ran a wide-toothed brush through my
hair. "I know, Mom. You don't have to remind me."

Mom rummaged through her bag until she pulled out her phone.
"Let me just call him."

"I don't need you guilting my own dad into spending time with me," I said.

"But, Bea," Mom started.

"I have to go. I'm meeting the girls." I grabbed my backpack and walked to the door.

"By 'girls,' I'm hoping Maisy's included," Mom said. "It was weird not having her here for our post-Halloween breakfast."

"You're obsessed with Maisy!" I said, feeling my cheeks getting pink as my voice rose.

"Bea." Mom's voice got softer. "You know all too well what it feels like to be left out."

"You think Maisy's so perfect, but she ditched me. Again. Only for a guy this time," I said, as I opened the door.

"Wait, Bea, let's talk about this," Mom said, burying her hands in her curls.

"I have to go. The girls are waiting for me at Mia's."

Mom walked over to me. She looked like she was about to hug me, then thought better of it. "I know this is going to be hard to believe, but I remember what it's like to be in middle school."

"Middle school was a different world back then," I said. "You had one of those phones with the curly cord."

Mom smirked. "Um, by the time I was in middle school we had a cordless phone with call-waiting."

"I don't even know what that means," I said. "You can't even begin to understand what it's like now."

Mom threw her hands up in the air. "Then help me understand. Don't push me away."

"I have to go," I said, and walked out the door.

Mom called after me, "I love you!"

I couldn't get away from her and her lectures fast enough. When I got to Mia's house, she ran over and gave me a big hug.

The other girls were lounging on the couch, but they all jumped up and greeted me like I mattered, like they really wanted to be with me. I finally felt like I didn't have to fight so hard to be a part of them. I started out the school year thinking they were the ones I was fighting to hold on to, when instead I had been fighting to keep Maisy all along.

"So glad you didn't have to hang out with your dad today," Madison said. "We have the best day planned."

Mia cut in. "My mom's friend just started a traveling beauty salon. She's using us as models for her website!"

"We're getting mani-pedis, facials, and blowouts," Madeline added.

"For free," Chloe added.

I smoothed my hair down. "That's amazing! I really need a blowout. This straightening treatment is growing out already."

"I can see that," Meghan said, reaching for a handful of my dry hair.

"We just have one problem," Mia said, with a pouty look and pleading voice.

"What?" I asked, with the sinking feeling that I was somehow the solution to the problem.

"We have to finish our take-home math midterms first," Mia said. "My mom is being a total nightmare about it. She won't let her friend come until we show her our finished tests."

I bit my bottom lip. "Helping with homework is one thing, but I don't know about a midterm. That could get us in a lot of trouble."

Madeline took a step back. "I don't want anything to do with this. I already finished mine, by myself, at home."

"Come on, Bea. It's no big deal. Do you know how many kids have tutors helping them? You're like our tutor," Mia said.

"Yeah," Madison said. "Everyone I know has a tutor."

"Or their mom does their work for them," Chloe said.

"You guys heard what Mr. Pembrook said. We aren't allowed to get any help from anyone or it's a strict honor code violation," Madeline said. "You guys are better off with a bad grade on a take-home midterm than getting busted for this."

I knew Madeline was right. I knew this was a really terrible idea. I was about to say no, I really was.

But then, Mia looked at me and said, "We need you, Bea. We really do."

And I realized the M & Ms were all I had. Mom had Mr. Pembrook. Dad had Monica and his new daughters. Maisy had Clark. All I had was the M & Ms, and I wasn't going to let them down.

"Let's see your tests," I said.

MAISY

I was reaching into my locker when I felt a tap on my back. I figured it had to be Clark since he was the only person talking to me these days. I whipped around with a big smile on my face.

But it was Chloe. Shockingly, she wasn't attached to Madison's hip.

"I just wanted to say sorry," Chloe whispered. She stood there clenching and unclenching her hands, and her nervous energy was contagious.

I slowly stood up, with a sinking feeling in my stomach. "For what?"

"You had my back at Halloween. I should've had yours," Chloe said, her eyes welling up. "I feel like such a jerk."

I folded my arms. "You're not the one who needs to apologize. Bea's the one who chose the M & Ms over me."

"But she didn't," Chloe said.

"Um, I think it's pretty obvious that she did," I said.

"You don't understand." Chloe twisted the Poppy Red scrunchie on her wrist. "She explained to the girls what's been going on with you."

I leaned in closer so I could really hear her. "What exactly did she say?"

"I'm sure everyone will understand if you just tell them you've been stressed because of your mom," Chloe said.

My chest tightened up and I felt like I couldn't take a deep breath. "Um, my mom?"

Chloe put her hand on my arm. "Bea told us about your mom's problem. I'm so sorry."

My ears were ringing with every word that came out of Chloe's mouth. "Bea told you guys? About my mom?"

Chloe's tone was sweet and sympathetic, which only made me feel worse. "You were so nice to me with the whole peanut allergy thing. I just want you to work things out."

It felt like Chloe was standing on the other side of a big wall and I couldn't hear her.

The bell rang, and everyone rushed down the hall, while I stood stuck right where I was.

"Sorry, can't be late to English again," Chloe said.

She ran down the hall before I could even say thank you.

I felt so stupid. How had I missed it all along? The only reason Bea had become friends with me again was because of the stupid pact. She was so desperate to be popular that she was willing to do anything, including betray me.

I walked into Mr. Pembrook's class feeling like my legs had cement blocks tied to them. I slumped into my seat and let my hair fall over my face.

Mr. Pembrook stood in front of us with a stack of midterms. "Today's the big day! Time to give the midterms back. Some of you did even better than expected. I just want to give a shout-out to Mia, Meghan, Madison, and Chloe for getting perfect scores."

George raised his hand. "Does that mess up the curve for the rest of us?"

Mr. Pembrook gave a sympathetic smile. "Yeah, it kinda does, because that means everyone else had to do a lot better than usual to get an A."

Madeline made eye contact with me for the first time since Halloween. She folded her arms and gave me a knowing look.

We both knew two things. Mia Atwater was not capable of getting a perfect score on a math midterm, and Madeline was the only one of the M & Ms who wasn't getting answers from Bea.

Mr. Pembrook walked around the room, putting midterms facedown on desks. When he got to me, he leaned down. "You did a great job on this test. If it were any other year, this would be a solid B plus. Don't let the curve get you down."

I flipped over my paper and saw a B minus circled in red at the top. Bea was seeping into every part of my life and ruining it.

I spent the rest of math class rage-doodling in my notebook. When the bell rang, I waited till the last of the kids left. Then I went up to Mr. Pembrook's desk.

"Maisy, I know you didn't get the grade you wanted because of the curve, but you should still be really proud of your work," Mr. Pembrook said. "I have seen great improvement in your skills since the first day of class."

I rubbed my sneaker back and forth on the tile. "Aren't you curious how those girls got perfect scores?"

Mr. Pembrook blinked at me. "What are you saying?"

"Mia, Meghan, Madison, and Chloe aren't capable of getting a perfect midterm grade. But they're friends with someone who is."

I turned on my heel and walked out of the classroom.

→⋯ CHAPTER TWENTY-THREE ⋯←

BEA

AFTER SCHOOL, MR. PEMBROOK AND I WALKED IN THE DOOR AT home just when Mom was heading out.

Mom slipped on her heels and wrangled her unruly curls into a topknot. "Such a crazy workweek. I think everyone's trying to finalize sales before the holidays."

Mr. Pembrook pulled out a stack of packets and sat down at the kitchen table. "I have a crazy week, too. I'm still trying to finish grading these so I can upload quarter grades to the portal."

My stomach sank. I had studied like crazy for my finals, but even with A's on all of them, my grades were still going to be hard to explain to Mom.

"I should be back super quick. The showing is only a few blocks from here." Mom blew kisses at us and hustled out the door just as her cell phone started ringing.

As soon as Mom left, Mr. Pembrook's smile and jovial tone were gone.

I turned to go upstairs. "I have to go get ready for Mia's."

Mr. Pembrook's tone was sharp. "Bea, sit down."

I sat down slowly.

He pulled off his reading glasses and folded them closed. "I'm worried about you."

"I studied really hard for Dr. Butterfield's midterm. He said if I can get an A on it, I can raise my class grade to passing," I said. "I've been coming in for extra help all week for all my midterms."

"I can see it's worse than I thought." Mr. Pembrook sighed. "But it's not just *your* tests I'm worried about."

What was that supposed to mean?

Mr. Pembrook pulled out a stack of papers from his messenger bag, and I immediately recognized the take-home midterm with Mia's handwriting on the top packet.

He spread the stack of pages like a hand of cards, and, in addition to Mia's test, I saw Meghan's, Madison's, and Chloe's.

"I have four take-home tests with identical answers on them," Mr. Pembrook said. "Four perfect scores."

"Okay," I said, trying to keep my tone even and a facial expression that said I had no idea what this had to do with me.

"This is the first time in my teaching career that I have had four perfect grades on a midterm," Mr. Pembrook continued.

I looked down at my hands clenched in my lap. "Aren't you break-ing some kind of confidentiality rule? I really don't feel comfortable talking about other students' grades."

"Stop playing games with me, Bea." Mr. Pembrook slapped the papers down on the table. "You know this is a violation of the honor code. We should be in the principal's office right now."

"How is it a violation to tutor people?" I asked.

"I think you know the difference between tutoring someone and giving all the answers," he said.

"I can't believe you're not giving me the benefit of the doubt! You know me. You're practically living at my house," I said.

"That's why we're talking *here* instead of in the principal's office." Mr. Pembrook tapped his finger on the stack of papers. "Usually, this happens when parents spend a fortune on tutors who do all the work for the kids. There's nothing I can really do about it. If you weren't giving these girls the answers, their parents would probably be pay-ing some adult who would. So I'm not that worried about them. *You,* on the other hand, you I *am* worried about."

As his tone softened, it only made me feel more defensive. I folded my arms across my chest. "Why are you so worried about me?"

"For starters, your grade in Dr. Butterfield's class. If you could get a perfect score on a midterm in my class, there's no way you should be in danger of failing honors math."

I breathed out. "You don't understand. Taking a full course load of honors classes is hard. Everything moves so much faster and there's so much homework. It's impossible to keep up."

"I think you've been spending so much time trying to make sure these girls pass their math class that you haven't been putting the time into studying for your very challenging honors classes," Mr. Pembrook said.

I swallowed hard, trying to think of a comeback.

Mr. Pembrook's tone softened again. "Your mom told me you had straight A's last year. What's going on now?"

I could feel my cheeks getting redder and redder as my voice rose. "I may have had perfect grades, but I also had no friends. No one to walk to school with. No one to sit at lunch with. No one to hang out with after school. Do perfect grades really matter if I hate my life?"

"I get it, Bea. I wasn't exactly Mr. Popularity myself in middle school," Mr. Pembrook said.

"Really?" I said. "That is so shocking."

"But I don't think this group of girls is worth what you're risking here." He paused. "And I'll ignore your sarcasm."

All of a sudden, the pieces came together, and I wanted nothing more than to run from the room, run from this conversation. But I had to know.

"It was Maisy, wasn't it?" I said. "Maisy told you."

Mr. Pembrook shook his head. "For such a smart kid, you're

focusing on the wrong things lately."

"Did you ever think it might be kind of hard for me to focus with you here all the time?"

Mr. Pembrook's whole body jolted back like I had smacked him in the face.

My anger was bubbling up to the surface and spewing all over him. "I'm already dealing with my dad getting married and adopting two girls I *barely* know. Maybe I'm going off the rails because, on top of that, you're practically living with us," I said.

He breathed in hard.

The words came out hot and fast. "You're with my mom all the time! I can't get her alone to talk about how I hate my new room at Dad's house or how awful I look in my bridesmaid dress or how it makes me uncomfortable to see you walking around my house in pajamas!"

Mr. Pembrook stood up. "Bea—"

I ran out of the house. But then I stopped and turned back and yelled, "And I hate oat milk!"

MAISY

I couldn't get out of school fast enough. I threw all my books in my backpack without even checking which ones I actually needed and ran out the door. I wanted to get as far away from school and this awful day as fast as possible.

As soon as I got close to my street, Addy FaceTimed me. She was holding the phone so close to her face that I could practically see her tonsils. I could hear the pounding of powerful gymnasts tumbling off the vault and the bars and the sounds of coaches shouting directions at them.

Words came pouring out of my mouth. "Are you hurt? What happened? Is it Mom?"

"Everything's good. You're always such a stress case." Addy's face broke out in a huge smile. "I landed my full-in double-back on the floor!"

"The move you need to make it to level ten?" I asked.

"Yes!" Addy shouted.

I jumped up and down on the sidewalk, and Addy jumped up and down at the gym.

"Want to see my floor routine?" Addy asked.

"Yes!" I said.

Addy passed the phone to Tashie, who waved at me before turning the phone on Addy.

As I watched Addy flip through the air and land on her two feet, only to leap back up again into another tumble pass, some of the bad feelings of the day started to melt away.

As soon as the music stopped, Addy rushed back over to the

phone. "What do you think?"

"You are definitely making level ten," I said.

"Gotta get back." Addy blew me a kiss, then the screen went black.

Watching Addy land those moves made me feel like maybe there was hope for everything else.

I shoved my phone back in my pocket and turned around toward my house.

"Aaaah!" I jumped back. "Bea! You scared me!"

"You told Mr. Pembrook?" she shouted, with her hands on her hips.

All of the good feelings I'd gotten from Addy drained right out of me. "I worked my butt off on that take-home test," I said. "You screwed up the curve!"

"I would've helped you, too." Bea took a step closer to me, and in lower voice, she said, "All you had to do was ask."

"Because I'm so dumb, right? Because there's no way I could do well in math without your help?"

Bea tilted her head in a condescending way. "No one's calling you dumb."

"I didn't need your help. I just needed you to not sabotage the curve!" I shouted.

"So I unintentionally mess up your curve, and you get revenge by intentionally telling on me?"

"At least I had a good reason," I said.

Bea threw her hands up. "What's that supposed to mean?"

"You told them! You told the girls about my mom."

Bea practically spit the words at me. "I was trying to help you!"

"By betraying me?"

"We all saw you," Bea said.

"What're you talking about?" I asked.

"In the chem lab with Clark. I should've known you were keeping secrets again," Bea said.

"I already told you about Clark's dad," I said.

"It's obvious you guys are dating and you're choosing *him* over *us*," Bea said. "All the girls say so."

"Since when are you and the M & Ms an US? What happened to you and me being the us?"

"We were an *us* until you ditched me last year!" Bea said.

"I thought we were past that!" I said.

"I thought we were, too, but once again you're choosing someone else over me," Bea said.

"I'm not choosing anyone over you. You're so obsessed with being an M & M that you're acting like a totally different person."

"Oh, so it was all right when you changed to be part of my friend group at camp, but not when it's my turn?"

"How can you even compare the Sunflower girls to the M & Ms? Why would you want to be friends with the M & Ms when you've seen what real friends are?" I asked.

"The Sunflower Bunk girls weren't here when I had no one to sit with at lunch," Bea said.

"The M & Ms are going to drop you as soon as they figure out how desperate you are. Then you'll be a loser all over again," I said.

"I'm not the one who has to worry about losing her seat at the popular table. I'm done trying to fix things for you," Bea said.

"If your idea of fixing things for me is betraying me, then I don't need your kind of help!" I turned on my heel and stormed away.

CHAPTER TWENTY-FOUR

BEA

I RODE MY BIKE AROUND THE NEIGHBORHOOD AMPED UP ON RAGE and adrenaline. I waited till I burned off most of my anger before I headed back home. By the time I got there, Mr. Pembrook's car was gone from the driveway, which was a relief because I was equal parts guilty and embarrassed for unloading on him, even though I had been right about everything I said.

When I walked in the kitchen, Mom, still wearing her work clothes, was sitting at the kitchen table with her forehead resting in the palms of her hands. The kettle was whistling and water was bubbling out of the spout.

I ran over to the stove and turned it off. "Mom? Are you okay?"

She lifted her head. Her eyes and nose were bright red and there were streaks of mascara under her eyes.

"Mom! What's going on?" I pulled up a chair next to her. "You're scaring me."

Mom wiped her eyes with the palms of her hands, then she pulled her curls up into a tight topknot. "I'm sorry, Bea. I was trying to get it together before you got home."

My stomach tightened. I hadn't seen her like this since Dad moved out. "What happened?"

Mom sniffed. "Gavin broke up with me."

"What? Did he say why?"

Mom shook her head. "I don't know what happened. He seemed fine just a few hours ago. Then, out of nowhere, he said he needs some space. He told me as soon as I got home, and then he left."

"It's going to be okay, Mom," I said, feeling guilt coursing through my veins. "I'll finish making that tea for you."

She grabbed a paper towel and blew her nose really loud. I put the steaming mug of tea in front of her.

"Thanks, Bea," Mom said. "I should be the one comforting you through a breakup, not the other way around."

Mom didn't need to hear about my Maisy drama right now.

"I need a distraction," she said. "Grades came out today, right?" She picked up her mug and took a long sip.

"Who cares about school at a time like this?"

Mom pulled out her phone and swiped her finger over the screen. "I need something to cheer me up."

"Before you—" I started.

But it was too late. Mom sucked in a deep breath, and even though it didn't seem possible, she looked even more distraught than she had when I first walked in the door.

"Bea?" Mom said, making my name sound like an accusation.

"It's not as bad as it looks," I said.

"C's in math, science, and social studies!" Mom said. "How could this not be bad?"

"I got an A in English and an A minus in Spanish," I countered.

"Those classes don't count. You came out of the womb practically reading Shakespeare, and you've always been gifted at Spanish. You can get A's in those classes without breaking a sweat."

"You're the one who thought the honors classes were too hard for me," I said. "I should've listened to you and dropped down."

"That's a cop-out and you know it. If you spent half the time studying that you do on your hair and makeup, you wouldn't be in this mess," Mom said.

"You don't understand, Mom," I said. "There's so much pressure now to look and be a certain way."

"I know you like these girls, and I get it. But I don't think they're helping you," Mom said. She pressed the hot mug on the spot between her eyes, which meant on top of everything else she was getting a migraine.

"This isn't about the M & Ms. I had a rough first quarter. I have three more quarters to raise my grades. I started going to extra help," I said.

"You don't need extra help. You just need to be focusing more on your schoolwork instead of hanging out with these superficial girls!" Mom said.

"So I can sit home with you every Friday night? You just want to hold me back so I'll be here with you all the time," I said.

"That's not true, and I think you know that," Mom said. "I just want you to have the right priorities."

"And you're the expert on priorities?" I shouted.

"What's that supposed to mean?"

"Maybe you would've noticed I was having trouble in school sooner if you weren't spending every second with your boyfriend," I said.

Mom put the mug back on the table, so I could see every inch of her face. She fixed her eyes on mine. "I'm going to have plenty of time to keep track of you and your schoolwork since Gavin won't be around. You are grounded until further notice."

MAISY

When I walked in the room, Addy was hanging up her competition leotard on the back of the closet door. Addy's pre-meet routine was always the same: She laid out her rhinestone-covered black, silver, and purple leotard and matching warm-up suit. Then she checked her bag for her grips, flip-flops, Tiger Paws, and hair kit with hair ties, scrunchies, and gel. She always had everything she needed, but she always checked at least three times.

I waited till her third check was complete, then asked, "Want me to do your hair for you?"

"Can you do the side braid across the top and connect it to a high pony?" she asked.

"Good choice. That brought you good luck at the last meet," I said.

I grabbed my hair gel, tiny rubber bands, fine-tooth comb, hairbrush, and hair spray. I had been styling Addy's hair for meets for the past two years. Mom stopped doing Addy's hair right around the same time she stopped sewing costumes.

Addy sat with perfect posture while I sprayed her hair with detangling spray.

"And make it extra tight," she said, while I combed through all the knots. "So it stays for tomorrow."

"I know," I said.

The only time Addy ever sat still was when I braided her hair for meets. It was the easiest time to talk to her.

"Are you nervous?" I asked, while I separated her hair into sections.

"Yes," Addy said. "I'm so worried about sticking that floor landing."

"You'll do it," I said. I could practically feel her nervous energy coming off her scalp. "Just try not to give in to all the pressure. Think about it like any other meet."

"How am I supposed to do that?"

My fingers moved across the top of Addy's scalp as I twisted the hair into a thick braid. "If your coach didn't think you were ready for this, you would know."

Addy sighed. "Thanks for backing off from the Mom situation. I just can't deal with any drama right now."

It was a good thing I had stuck the end of the comb in my mouth, because all I had to do was nod.

Hours later, Addy's snores filled the room. She had tucked herself in as soon as I finished her hair so she would get a good night's sleep. You would think her nerves would keep her awake, but her body was so tired from training that she always fell asleep within minutes of her head hitting the pillow. Kind of like my days training for the tournament at Camp Amelia.

I looked at my phone. It was one a.m. If I didn't get some sleep, I was going to be a mess at the meet. How could I sleep when my life was falling apart? Not to mention my stomach was growling because I was too stressed out to eat dinner earlier.

I quietly pushed my blankets back and climbed down my

loft-bed ladder. I tiptoed across the room and nudged the door open. When I walked past Mom and Dad's room, I could hear Dad snoring. I walked downstairs carefully, avoiding the squeaky middle step.

In the kitchen, I filled a big bowl full of Lucky Charms. Then I picked through the box for extra marshmallows and put them on top. I was just pouring the milk when I heard a crackle come from outside.

My heart started beating super fast as my mind ran through the list of things that would make that sound, which included bears that might know how to open our back door and burglars like the guys in *Home Alone*.

Suddenly, the back doorknob rattled. I ducked down under the kitchen island and scrunched into a tight ball, making myself as small as possible. I was trying to figure out what Kevin McCallister would do in this situation when I saw Mom's feet walking across the kitchen floor. Instead of feeling relieved that we weren't being robbed, I almost felt worse. I tucked myself in tighter so Mom wouldn't spot me and prayed that she wouldn't notice the cereal on the counter.

I watched as her bare feet paced back and forth across the cold kitchen floor. Then the sound of her dialing her phone broke the silence. I heard it ring, once, twice. On the third ring, someone picked up.

"It's me," Mom said.

The only person Mom could be calling in the middle of the night ... the only other person who might be awake was someone who could get her some pills. I heard the glass door slide open as she headed back out onto the back patio to finish her conversation.

I slid out from under the island and headed back upstairs. All I wanted to do was wake Dad up. But we all had to be up early for Addy's meet. I wasn't going to be the one to screw this up for Addy. As soon as the meet was over I was going to tell him I had been right about Mom all along.

CHAPTER TWENTY-FIVE

BEA

MOM AND I DON'T GET INTO ARGUMENTS. SOMETIMES WE GET ON each other's nerves and get a little snippy with each other, but yesterday was our first big blowout fight.

Mom ran into the kitchen and slipped her feet into her heels while she tucked in her shirt. Her wet curls dripped down the back of her shirt, she had dark circles under her eyes, and she looked paler than usual.

"We still have some things to talk about. I really wouldn't leave if I didn't have this huge open house today," Mom said, while she slung her gigantic work bag over her shoulder.

"It's fine, Mom. I'm going to be catching up on schoolwork all day." I tapped my pencil on my math textbook for emphasis.

Mom breathed out hard and fast. "I'm sorry, Bea. I should've noticed before things got so out of control."

I felt a surge of guilt roll through my stomach. "It's not your fault."

"I have to go. There are leftovers in the fridge for dinner if I'm not home in time. We'll talk more later, okay?"

I nodded.

Mom kissed the top of my head on her way out the door. Just when I thought she left, she poked her head back in. "There's terrible cell reception up in Maple Hills. So you might not be able to reach me."

"Don't worry. Mr. Pebbles and I will be fine while you're gone," I said, waving her out the door.

As soon as Mom closed the door, I slammed my math book shut and pulled out my phone and texted the M & Ms.

From: Bea
To: Mia, Madeline, Meghan, Madison, Chloe

Come now

Twenty minutes later, we were all huddled around the sink at Bath & Body Works trying out sugar scrubs in the middle of their semiannual sale chaos. I quickly realized shopping therapy is a very real thing.

"Which one?" Madison held both of her sugar scrub–covered hands up to my nose. "Watermelon Lemonade or Sun-Washed Citrus?"

"The one on the left," I said, relishing in the simple question.

Chloe nodded. "Agreed."

"Watermelon Lemonade." Madison nodded, her mouth set in a very serious expression. "I thought so."

"Look, they have the Poppy Red lip gloss!" Mia held up a tube of the shade of lip gloss everyone had been borrowing from me.

"But it's seven dollars," Chloe said. "I really wanted to get a bath bomb from Lush and I'm almost out of money."

"Mia can solve that problem," Meghan said.

One second the lip gloss was in Mia's hand, the next, it was in her pocketbook. "They're so busy in here, no one's gonna notice," she said.

I looked around us, convinced one of the saleswomen wearing a blue canvas apron would come running over and tackle Mia to the ground. But they were all so busy grabbing shopping totes for customers, ringing them up, and putting more body washes and lotions out on display that no one even gave us a second look.

Madeline tucked a lip gloss into her denim jacket sleeve. "They overcharge for everything in here. That covers things like this."

Meghan tucked a lip gloss in the waistband of her leggings and let her sweatshirt fall over it. "So easy," she said.

Madison and Chloe looked at each other with wide eyes. Madison gave Chloe a barely perceptible nod. Then Madison slipped a lip gloss into her sweatshirt pocket, and Chloe dropped hers in her pocketbook.

My heart was pounding. I scanned the store for anyone who would bust us. But the other customers were keeping the saleswomen so busy that they looked like they barely had time to breathe let alone look around for petty thieves.

"Follow me," Mia said.

I clenched my hands into tight fists as we walked out of the store. I braced myself for the alarm to go off. I looked from right to left, ready for a security guard to come out of nowhere and use the Taser on us. But nothing happened.

As soon as we got a few stores down, Meghan shrieked, "How easy was that?"

"So easy," Chloe said.

"I got such an adrenaline rush!" Madeline said.

Mia looked at me with narrowed eyes. "You didn't take one, Bea."

"I already have that color. Let's go in the pop-up beauty supply store," I said, in an attempt to distract from the fact that I was the only one who hadn't risked getting into trouble.

The Beauty Influencer, which used to be a Pretzel Time, still smelled like pretzel-covered hot dogs, but it looked sleek with the all-white walls and stainless steel shelves that showcased makeup, brushes and applicators, and hair-styling tools.

A twenty-something saleswoman greeted us as soon as we walked in the empty store. Her blond hair hung in beachy waves down her back, and her face looked both natural and fully made up at the same time. She was cleaning the demo makeup brushes.

"Ten percent off foundation and concealers today," she said.

"Thanks," I said, with a friendly smile.

The saleswoman turned back to the makeup counter and continued cleaning the demo brushes. "Let me know if you girls need anything."

Mia went right to the lip-plumping gloss.

Two seconds later she waved her hands over her mouth, like she had just eaten Flamin' Hot Cheetos.

"OMG! My lips are stinging!" she shouted.

"That goes away in about fifteen minutes," the saleswoman called over.

"Fifteen minutes?!" Mia shouted.

Madison and Chloe put down the lip-plumping gloss they had been about to try.

"But do my lips look bigger?" Mia asked, turning to all of us with her lips in a duckie position.

"Not really," Meghan said.

"My mom says those things don't work," Madeline said.

"Maybe you need to give it a little more time," I said in a reassuring tone.

Meghan held up a bottle of lotion that promised to make freckles disappear. "Do you think this works?"

Madeline grabbed the bottle and looked underneath it. "For a hundred dollars, it better."

"You need one of these, Bea." Mia picked up a cordless flat iron. "Your hair's starting to frizz up at the roots."

She was right. The keratin treatment was growing out, and my curls were coming back with a big, puffy vengeance. With Maisy and Mom mad at me, I had no hope of getting another keratin treatment anytime soon.

I flipped over the price tag. "It's two hundred and fifty dollars."

Mia looked at the saleswoman, who was now on the phone with what sounded like a vendor, complaining about her latest shipment of round hairbrushes.

Mia whispered, "You saw how easy it is."

Madeline looked at her with wide eyes and hissed, "That was lip gloss."

I looked over at the saleswoman, certain she must be able to hear us, but her voice was rising to a crescendo as she yelled about the difference between boar bristles and metal-pronged brushes.

"Take the sample," Meghan said. "It's so small. You can fit it in your bag, no prob."

"She won't even notice," Madison said.

"She's too busy reaming someone out on the phone," Chloe said.

"We'll cover you," Madeline said.

The girls flanked around me and pretended to be looking at curling wands.

Mia looked at me with wide eyes that said, "Come on, do it."

I felt a surge of adrenaline as I wrapped my hands around the flat iron. I dropped it in my open bag.

The girls were right. This was so easy.

"Come on, girls, let's go to the food court," Mia said, in an unnatural voice.

The girls moved in a pack to the wide store exit. I closed my bag and followed right behind them. My heart felt like it was pounding out of my chest, and my tongue was so dry I could barely swallow.

I had one foot still in the store, and one foot out, when the saleswoman shouted, "Stop! Thief!"

My feet froze, like they were stuck in mud and I couldn't will my body to move.

Mia grabbed Madeline's arm and yelled, "Run!"

I stood rooted to the spot as all the M & Ms ran away from the store. I watched them sprint away at top speed down the hallway, leaving me alone with a stolen flat iron in my bag.

MAISY

"Hurry up, Eddy," Grandma said, while she pumped her arms and walked at her fastest walking pace. "We want good seats."

Dad chuckled. "Relax, Mom. You'll be able to see just fine wherever we sit."

"As long as no one tall sits in front of me," Grandma said.

While Grandma went on a rant about tall people always sitting in front of the shortest person in the room, I was shoveling Sour Patch Kids in my mouth as fast as I could. I needed the sugar to wake up. My eyes were dry and my head was throbbing, and the last place I wanted to be was at a gymnastics meet.

We followed the crowd down the hall into the Five Rivers High School gym. The floors were covered with springboards for the floor routines and there were two sets of bars, beams, and vaults. I settled into the wooden bleachers, ready for a long day.

As soon as she sat down, Grandma panned her phone around as she videoed for her Instagram story. "Just look at this crowd for the first USA Gymnastics meet of the season!"

"This gym is kind of small." Mom pulled at a loose thread on her sleeve and rubbed it between her fingers. "Addy doesn't like smaller venues. She says it makes her more anxious when she can see the faces in the crowd."

Dad put his hand on Mom's back. "Addy's going to be fine. She's been competing at meets like this since first grade. It doesn't matter what kind of venue she's in. She always kicks butt."

"A little anxiety isn't going to hurt. She could use some of that adrenaline for her floor routine. There are a lot of power moves in the choreography," Grandma, the gymnastics expert, said.

Mom started picking at the pale pink gel polish on her thumbnail. "Maybe she's putting too much pressure on herself. I mean, does she really need to qualify for level ten after one level-nine meet?"

"Isn't that the reason you let her homeschool?" Grandma reminded her. "So that she can get to level ten at this meet and qualify for Junior Elite by the end of the season?"

"But does it have to be on that timeline?" Mom asked.

"If she wants a shot at the Olympics, it does," I said.

"I'm starving." Mom jumped up. "Does anyone want anything from the snack bar?"

"Can you get me a coffee?" Grandma asked.

"Make that two," Dad said.

"Want anything, Maisy?" Mom asked.

I shook my head.

"Hurry back!" Grandma called. "You don't want Addy looking up and seeing you're not here."

"I'll be quick," Mom said.

She ran down the bleacher steps, but she looked shaky and off balance. Her foot caught on the edge of a bleacher and she fell forward. She reached out her arms and fell into a big man, who dropped his bagel.

"I'm so sorry," she said.

"It's okay," he said, but he was clearly annoyed.

Mom stood back up and rushed down the stairs, even more wobbly this time.

I looked over at Dad, but he didn't seem to notice how weird Mom was acting. Grandma whipped out her phone and started another recording. "The meet is about to start and the girls are using every last second to warm up their muscles and stretch out."

She focused in on Addy's team, who were all lined up doing their stretching routine. If they were nervous, they didn't show it. These girls had been competing all their lives and they knew how to look confident, even when they were scared.

"Show our shirts, Mom." Dad smoothed down the front of his T-shirt. A few years ago, Mom had made us all T-shirts with a picture of Addy on the front and her team on the back.

Grandma zoomed in on Dad's shirt. "We have the most spirit in this crowd."

Then Grandma switched her phone to selfie mode. "Signing off for now. Will be back again with some live event coverage."

Dad laughed. "Maybe you can have a second career in sports broadcasting, Mom."

Mom ran back to the bleachers with a tray full of coffees. She still looked wobbly walking up the steps but managed to get back to us without spilling coffee everywhere.

"Perfect timing," Dad said, reaching for his coffee. "Addy's up next on the bars."

If you were wondering where the expression "sitting on the edge of their seats" came from, I think it came from someone watching a gymnastics meet. We all slid as far forward as we could, to the edge of our seats, and clasped our hands together, kind of in prayer, but also to keep our hands from shaking. Dad always says he's done more praying at gymnastics meets than at church over the years.

Addy's team competed on bars first. Addy hopped up onto the low bar and she looked like a superhero as she flipped over the bars again and again, twisting her body in impossible ways. I didn't realize I was holding my breath until she flipped off the high bar, twisted and tumbled, and landed on both of her feet.

I looked at Mom. Tears streamed down her face as she gripped Dad's hand and whispered to him, "I almost missed this."

Dad whispered back, "But you didn't. I'm so proud of you."

I didn't realize I was chewing on the inside of my lip until I tasted blood.

Grandma turned to me. "Your sister's on her way to the Olympics."

Addy's beam and vault routines were just as solid as her bars, proving Grandma right.

When Addy's team lined up to compete on floor, Mom's anxiety kicked into overdrive again. I could feel her nervous energy shedding off her body. She tapped her leg so fast and hard that it made the bleacher row shake. But even Dad, who is used to keeping his cool at work, kept running his fingers through his hair, his tell that he was freaking out on the inside.

Mom was shaking her leg so hard that her big bag toppled over. It felt like everything toppled out in slow motion. First came her makeup bag, then came the leather wallet Dad got her for her birthday, then came a plastic car container of Spearmint gum that rattled as it flew through the air.

Last came a bottle of pills.

Everything around me went black. All I could see was the bottle of pills rolling down the bleachers into the next row.

"I knew it!" I jumped up out of my seat. "I knew it! I knew it this whole time!"

Mom covered her mouth with one hand and reached her other hand out to me.

The words couldn't come out of my mouth fast enough or loud enough. "*Everyone* else believed you! But that's because you are such a good liar. I was the only person who knew you hadn't changed!"

"Maisy, don't do this," Mom pleaded, her face red, while the man she had tripped over earlier walked up the steps and handed her the bottle of pills without making eye contact.

I turned to Dad and Grandma. "No one believed me! Everyone treated me like I was crazy!"

Dad said, quietly, "Maisy, sit down. Please don't do this here."

I turned back to Mom. "I'm the only one who got it! I'm the only one who knew that you never wanted to stop. Not even after you almost drove off the bridge with Addy and me in the car!"

Dad put his hand on my arm and leaned in so close that I could feel his hot breath on my ear. "Maisy, that's your mom's medicine. It was prescribed by her recovery specialist. You can check the bottle if you don't believe me."

My ears were ringing and my head was pounding. My breath felt hot and sour. Everyone was staring at me as the blackness faded, and I registered the Ariana Grande song playing in the background— Addy's floor routine music. I looked out on the floor and there was my sister, her face bright red as she flipped through the air and landed on her butt.

CHAPTER TWENTY-SIX

BEA

THE SALESWOMAN LOOKED AT ME OVER HER PHONE SCREEN. "Mall's closing in half an hour. If someone doesn't come and pay for this, I have to call the cops."

I stared at my phone, but nothing had changed since two seconds ago. Mom hadn't returned my calls or texts. I was out of options, so I took a deep breath and dialed.

My foot bounced up and down as the phone rang. He probably wouldn't answer. I wouldn't, if I were him.

But on the third ring, I heard, "Bea?"

I tried to speak but instead started crying uncontrollably.

Mr. Pembrook's voice was calm, but underneath I could hear worry. "Take a deep breath. It's going to be okay."

"I . . . I . . ." I didn't know how to tell him I'd been busted for shoplifting.

Mr. Pembrook's voice sounded more firm. "You need to tell me what's going on so I can help."

"Can you . . . can you . . ." I tried desperately to catch my breath.

"What? What do you need me to do?" Mr. Pembrook asked.

I pushed the words out between snorts and sobs. "Can you come to the . . . the mall?"

"The mall's a pretty big place. Can you narrow it down for me?" he asked.

"The pop-up beauty supply store, next to the Gap," I said.

I heard keys jangling and it sounded like he was walking fast. "On my way. What's going on, Bea?"

"I got caught." The word stuck in my throat. "Shoplifting a f-f-flat iron."

Mr. Pembrook drew in a sharp breath that whistled over the phone. "Did you do it?"

I swallowed hard. Of course he wasn't going to help. "Yes."

"I'll be there in ten minutes. Hang tight and don't say anything while you wait."

"Your dad coming?" the saleswoman huffed.

I nodded without bothering to correct her.

Eight minutes later, Mr. Pembrook came running into the store.

"Hi, I'm Rachelle. So nice to meet you," the saleswoman purred.

Mr. Pembrook reached out and shook her hand. "I'm Gavin."

Apparently, Mom wasn't the only one who found Mr. Pembrook cute. Rachelle was salivating over him.

"Thank you soooo much for coming," she said.

"Thank you for giving Bea the chance to call me," Gavin said. "I'm really hoping we can work something out."

Rachelle nodded, with a smile. "Oh, I'm sure we can work something out."

Mr. Pembrook turned to me. "What happened, Bea?"

"I'll show you." Rachelle pulled out her iPad. "See here she is hanging out with her friends. Then your daughter walked over to the display area and stuffed the flat iron in her bag."

Mr. Pembrook didn't bother correcting her either. He was too busy looking disappointed in me.

"Bea, did you apologize?"

"Y-yes," I said, even though Rachelle didn't own the Beauty Influencer. It's not like the flat iron cost was coming out of her paycheck either. "And I gave it back."

"So then, can I take her home? We are going to talk about how wrong this is," Mr. Pembrook said.

Rachelle smoothed down her shirt. "There's just one problem. This was a display flat iron. And now it's all messed up."

Mr. Pembrook held up the flat iron, then turned it over in his hands. "It looks fine to me. Let's turn it on to make sure it works."

Rachelle snatched it back. "It works, but I might need to spend a little to tighten the display cord. And if I have to do that, then I have to report it to corporate. If I report it to corporate, they'll want a police report."

Mr. Pembrook nodded. "I see. And how much will it cost to fix this?"

"The flat iron retails for two hundred, but we can settle on one fifty," she said. "Cash."

Mr. Pembrook didn't even blink. He pulled his wallet out of his back pocket and handed her a few bills. "There you go."

Then he put his hand on my shoulder. "Since we're all straightened out, we're gonna go."

He gave me a pointed look.

I took a deep breath. "I am so sorry for stealing the flat iron. I know you don't believe me, but it's the first time I ever did something like this." I looked down at the ground.

I followed Mr. Pembrook out of the mall, past the salespeople pulling down metal gates and locking up.

"I'll pay you back," I said. "I have a bunch of Christmas and birthday money saved."

Mr. Pembrook nodded.

"Thank you for coming," I said, while I walked fast to keep up with him. "My mom's at an open house with bad cell reception."

Mr. Pembrook looked at me closely. "So Maisy and all the girls left you?"

"Not Maisy. She wasn't with us."

"Lately, when I see you guys in the halls, Maisy's often not with you. Why is that?" Mr. Pembrook asked.

"She changed," I said. "It's like she isn't even trying to fit in with us."

Mr. Pembrook said, "That's odd. Because you're the one who looks like a different person."

MAISY

After meets, Addy always comes running over to us, her medals bouncing on her chest, a proud smile on her face. But this time, as soon as the awards ceremony ended, she ripped her three medals off right away and shoved them in her gym bag. The only thing that mattered was the 7.8 she got on floor, which kept her from qualifying for level ten. The 7.8 that was all my fault.

I waited for Addy to finish talking to Coach Tracy. It didn't look like the conversation went well because my sister, who never cries, not even the time she broke her arm after landing a move wrong on the balance beam, had tears streaming down her cheeks when she headed toward me.

"Addy," I pleaded, my hand reaching for her.

But she shoved past me, with her gym bag hitting me in the ribs. "Don't!" she said, and took off down the hall.

"Addy! Wait." I started to run after her, but then felt a firm hand on my shoulder.

"Give your sister some space," Dad said.

I felt like all I had done since I got home from camp was give everyone in my family space. I had spent the past few months on my own little island worrying about Mom all by myself.

I pulled away from him. "I need to talk to her. I need to tell her how sorry I am."

"This isn't about what you need right now," Dad said. "Come on, let's go to the car. Your sister will talk when she's ready."

Mom and Grandma followed silently behind us. I kept my face down so I wouldn't have to look at the other parents and gymnasts walking past us. A few minutes later, we were all crammed in Dad's car, but I still felt alone. The sound of Dad's blinker practically echoed through the quiet Jeep. Grandma sat between Addy and me, and neither one of them would look at me.

Addy threw her head back. "We're getting stuck at every. Single. Red. Light!"

"We'll be home soon." Grandma put her hand on Addy's knee. "It's okay."

Addy pushed her hand away. "It's not okay!"

Dad cut in with his calm voice. "There's another qualifying meet in a month. You'll have another shot then."

"That gives Tashie and Sage a month to get ahead of me with their training. My life is ruined!" Addy said.

"I know it feels that way right now—" Mom started.

"Don't start talking like a therapist," Addy said. "I had a plan, and Maisy sabotaged it."

Dad tried to catch Addy's eye in the rearview mirror. "I'm so sorry, sweetie. This is a bump in the road, you're going to make level ten. You just need another shot."

"I don't need another shot," Addy said. "I need to be an only child."

Grandma started doing the sign of the cross over her face. "Don't say that!"

"I'm sorry, Addy—" I started.

Addy leaned over Grandma. "I begged you to stop!" she said.

"I'm only trying to protect you!" I said.

"By ruining my gymnastics career?" Addy spat out.

"I didn't do it on purpose," I said. "You know that."

"The one thing I asked you to do was to stop obsessing about Mom," Addy said.

"Just because those pills were prescription doesn't mean Mom is clean," I said.

Dad pulled into the driveway. "What're you talking about?"

"I was in the kitchen last night when Mom made a secret late-night phone call," I said. "Who do you think she was calling?"

Mom unclicked her seat belt and turned around so I could see her. "My sponsor. I couldn't sleep because I was nervous about Addy's meet."

"So you ruined my meet over nothing?" Addy shouted.

I opened my mouth to speak, but she wasn't done yet.

"You *knew* how important this meet was to me and you ruined it!" Addy said.

I undid my seat belt so I could look over at her. "I didn't mean to, Addy. I swear!"

Addy glared at me. "You messed everything up!"

"If I could take it back, I would."

"You told me you stopped spying on Mom." Addy practically spat the words at me. "You promised."

Dad breathed out long and hard. "Maisy, I thought all that therapy at camp helped this summer."

Then he turned to Mom. "I knew we should've pushed the therapy issue when she came home."

"So Mom's the one who messed up and I have to get therapy?"

Mom sighed. "Therapy isn't a punishment, Maisy. I thought you realized that after getting to know Dr. Beth."

"It's always all about Maisy," Addy said. "Maisy's anxiety. Maisy

273

being mad at Mom. Maisy not wanting to go to camp. This was the one day that was supposed to be about *me*."

"I'm sorry," I said. "If Mom wasn't acting so weird, this never would've happened."

"Mom's not the one who screamed like a crazy person in the middle of my routine!" Addy yelled. "You can't keep blaming *everything* on Mom."

"This is my fault," Mom said. "I'm the one—"

Dad put his hand on her leg. "Let's table this discussion for now. It's been a rough morning. I think we need to have a little space before we talk some more."

Addy threw her door open and ran to the front door. Grandma followed as soon as she was able to get herself out of the Jeep. Mom and Dad walked behind them. No one said anything when I didn't get out of the car.

CHAPTER TWENTY-SEVEN

BEA

I SPENT THE FIRST FIVE MINUTES OF THE CAR RIDE STARING OUT the window. But as we got closer to my house, I knew I needed to say something.

"Thank you for rescuing me," I said. "I would probably be down at the Mapleton police station if you hadn't come."

"That's why I gave you my number," he said. "I meant what I said about being there if you needed me."

"I'm sorry about you and Mom." As the words came out of my mouth, I realized that I actually meant them.

Mr. Pembrook pressed his lips together, and his voice was gruff. "Me too."

As he drove up our street, he gripped the steering wheel tighter when he saw Mom's car pulling down the street at the exact same time.

Mom jumped out of the car with a big smile on her face when she saw Mr. Pembrook pull into the driveway.

She ran over to him, with her curls flowing in the wind behind her like she was in a movie. "Gavin!"

My heart lurched as I realized she thought he was here to get back together with her. I knew I should get out of the car and face her right away, but I stayed hunched in my seat like a coward, while Mr. Pembrook walked over to her.

Her face crumpled as he got closer to her with his own grim expression. I couldn't hear what he said, but there was no missing Mom yelling, "What?"

Mr. Pembrook walked back to the car and opened my door.

"I did the hard part for you," Mr. Pembrook said.

I heaved out a big sigh.

Mr. Pembrook waved his hand toward Mom, who was standing in the middle of the driveway with her arms folded across her chest. "Now all you have to do is get out of the car."

My torso felt like it was superglued to the car seat. "I can't face her. Not after what I've done," I whispered.

"Your mom's obviously not very happy with your behavior, but she loves you no matter what," Mr. Pembrook said.

I knew that couldn't be true, but I didn't want to waste any more of Mr. Pembrook's time, so I unclicked my seat belt.

"Thank you." I got out of the car. "For everything."

As soon as Mr. Pembrook pulled away, I crumpled down in the middle of the driveway. I didn't even care that I was sitting in the old oil stain or that there was a piece of asphalt digging into my calf.

"I don't know what's wrong with me," I cried.

Mom ran over and sat down next to me on the ground even though she was wearing her nice work clothes. She let out a big breath. "Oh, Bea."

The words came tumbling out. "I messed everything up. Maisy hates me. My grades suck. I almost got arrested for shoplifting. The M & Ms aren't really my friends. All that work trying to fit in with them and they left me! None of this was worth it." I swallowed hard. "Worst of all, I let you down."

Mom smoothed down my hair. "All of this is fixable. I know it doesn't seem like it, but it is."

"No, it's not." I rubbed my tears away with the back of my hand. "I screwed up so bad. There's no coming back from this."

Mom pushed my hair out of my face and put both of her hands on my cheeks, forcing me to look at her. "Do you honestly think you're the first middle schooler to make mistakes like this?"

"I don't know anyone else at school who has made such a mess of things," I said.

"How would you know? People don't post their mistakes all over Instagram," Mom said. "It's not like there's a #middleschoolmessups."

"But even if the whole world has screwed up as bad as me, it doesn't help me get my life back. I just feel like everything is so out of control, like my world is spinning out of control," I said.

Mom shook her head. "I should've realized what was going on before it got this bad. I was so wrapped up in Gavin that I missed all the signs."

I rubbed my nose with my shirt sleeve. "It's not your fault. You deserve to be happy."

Mom wiped away the tears that were streaming down my cheeks. "It's not too late to get you back on track. Let's tackle each of these situations one at a time."

I took a deep breath. "Okay. I can do that."

"Let's start with the shoplifting," Mom said.

"I told Mr. Pembrook I would pay him back with my Christmas and birthday money," I said.

"That's a start. You are also going to volunteer at the soup kitchen in Sugar Grove every Saturday for the next eight weeks," Mom said. "You need to spend some time looking outside of yourself and your little middle school bubble. Maybe helping people who really need it will help you to focus on the right things again."

I nodded. "Okay."

"You need to figure out how to get your grades back up," Mom said.

"I can go in for extra help every day, and I can come straight home after school and sit at the kitchen table until I've done all my homework and studying," I said.

"Sounds like a good plan," Mom said. "And I will check in to the portal more often."

I nodded. "You don't trust me anymore. I get it."

"Just because I didn't check on you doesn't mean I shouldn't have," Mom said. "I think we're both adjusting to middle school."

I stood up and stretched. "Can we go inside now?"

"We still haven't figured out how you're going to fix things with Maisy," Mom said.

"I don't think I can fix things with her," I said.

"Let's go inside and you can think about it while you try on your bridesmaid dress," Mom said. "We need to make sure it fits. The wedding's tomorrow and you haven't even tried it on."

I groaned as I stood up. "Maybe this dress is my punishment."

MAISY

The meet had ended hours ago and I didn't leave my room, even after Dad and Grandma convinced Addy to get out of the house and go with them to the movies to get her mind off everything. I think he was hoping if they all left, Mom and I would talk, but that was never going to happen. I was going to have to hide out in my room all week-end like I was now, snuggled up in the corner of the loft bed with my headphones on so I couldn't see or hear anyone.

Suddenly, Bea's head popped over the loft's edge.

"Ahhhh!" I yelled. "You scared me. You look like a zombie!" I shrieked.

Black lines of mascara trailed down her face and her hair was frizzy at the roots, like all it wanted was to be curly again. She had lipstick smeared on her chin, and one of her eyebrows still had liner on it, while the other one must've rubbed off so it looked like she only had one eyebrow.

"You were right about everything," Bea cried. She climbed into the top bunk with me wearing her hot pink bridesmaid dress.

I pulled my earbuds out. "Um, you're probably the only person in the world who thinks that right now."

"It's true. You really were right," Bea cried. "I never should've let Monica buy me this dress. Mr. Pembrook broke up with Mom, and it's all my fault. The M & Ms are horrible people, and I don't know how I ever thought I could be friends with them. And I'm practically failing seventh grade."

"Um, I don't even know where to start. And I can't stop looking at that dress," I said. Bea's hair looked like it was on fire against the hot pink mess that was swallowing her whole.

"I just need you not to hate me right now. I was selfish and a horrible friend and I didn't really get what that feels like until the M & Ms ditched me after I was caught shoplifting," Bea said.

"Wait. What?" I almost choked on my gum. "You were shoplifting?"

"I got caught shoplifting a flat iron at that beauty pop-up in the mall," Bea practically whispered.

"Let me guess . . . you were trying to impress Mia?" I asked.

She nodded. "I got caught and all the girls left me. If it wasn't for Mr. Pembrook, I would probably be sitting in jail right now."

I shook my head. "I never should've helped you be friends with them. I knew it was a mistake."

"It wasn't your fault." Bea groaned. "I'm a monster who can't be trusted to live in society. Can you please be my friend again? I need you."

"I'm pretty much a monster, too. My whole family hates me right now," I said.

Bea looked at me with wide eyes. "Why?"

"I made a huge scene at Addy's meet and accused my mom of doing drugs while Addy was in the middle of her floor routine. Spoiler alert: I was wrong *and* Addy screwed up her routine and didn't qualify for level ten."

"It's official." Bea started wailing. "We really can't handle not being friends!"

"Agreed," I said, feeling tears stream down my face.

I reached for Bea and it felt so good for her to hug me back. We stayed like that until we both stopped crying.

I wiped the tears off my face and sniffled. "Now can we talk about this dress?"

"I don't know how I'm going to walk down the aisle in this monstrosity. It's hideous," Bea said.

"Maybe we can fix it somehow," I said.

"The wedding's tomorrow. We don't have time," Bea cried.

Mom walked in the room. "Girls, I couldn't help overhearing . . ."

I folded my arms across my chest. "You mean eavesdropping."

Bea rubbed her face with the palms of her hands. "It's okay. I'm being really loud and dramatic."

Mom took a step closer to the loft bed, slowly, like we were both rabid animals. "I think I can help."

I held my hand up. "We're fine, Mom."

Bea waved her hands at herself. "You may be fine, Maisy. But I am very clearly not fine. How can you help?"

Mom adjusted her reading glasses on top of her head. "Come down so I can get a better look."

Bea looked like an extra from an eighties movie prom scene where there was some kind of mix-up at the dress store and her arch enemy had a hand in making her wear the worst possible dress for her complexion and body type.

Mom walked around Bea and chewed on her thumbnail. She put her reading glasses on and took a closer look at the hem. "I can fix this for you," she said.

Bea put her hands on her chest and breathed in sharply. "Can you really?"

Mom wrinkled her nose. "I have one question. How much can I change the dress?"

"Anything. Everything. Just do whatever you can to make me actually look pretty for my dad's wedding," Bea said.

"Are you sure?" Mom asked. "Because I have some ideas."

"I want to hold my own up there next to my new, beautiful stepsisters. I want to look pretty, but like me and not like a carbon copy of them," Bea said.

"I'll be right back," Mom said. "I just need to get some pins."

"Are you crazy?" I hissed as soon as Mom left the room.

"I'm taking your advice and trying to be myself around Monica and Dad, starting with wearing a bridesmaid dress that works for me, not for my Amazonian soon-to-be stepsisters."

"Be yourself—that's awesome! But are you really going to trust my mom with your dress? You'll end up with pant legs where the arm holes are supposed to be, or even worse, the whole bottom sewed up."

"You're never going to know for sure, unless you give her a chance. A real one," Bea said.

CHAPTER TWENTY-EIGHT

BEA

MAISY PACED BACK AND FORTH SO MANY TIMES I WAS SURPRISED she hadn't worn away the carpet tread.

"I'm the one who should be nervous," I said, reaching out and grabbing her arms to get her to stay in one place. "It's *my* dress."

"But what if my mom messed it up for you?" Maisy drifted off and looked down at the carpet. "I should never have let you do this."

"The dress couldn't get any worse," I said.

"That's the only thing saving you right now," Maisy said, snapping her gum manically.

"What if she actually did make it better?" I asked.

Maisy wrinkled her forehead. "What do you mean?"

"Well, if she did a good job on my dress, then would you take it as a sign that she's doing better?" I asked. "Maybe it's her way of showing you that you can trust her again."

Maisy didn't answer.

Her mom walked into the living room sipping an oversized mug of coffee. She was wearing the same relaxed jeans and black T-shirt from the day before and her hair was thrown up in the mother of all buns. "Your dress is hanging up on the back of the bathroom door. Try it on and then come show us."

Maisy stood there awkwardly with her mom while I headed to the bathroom.

When I opened the door, I gasped. It looked like Mrs. Winters had gone to a designer boutique and swapped out my dress for a new one.

"Hurry up!" called Maisy. "I'm dying to see it!"

I shrugged off my clothes and slipped into the dress. Mrs. Winters had solved the strapless problem by sewing transparent plastic straps to the bodice, so the dress was held safely in place, while still looking strapless. She had taken the dress up a few inches, so that it fell right below my knees, a length that even the clumsiest person in the world wouldn't trip over. But there was one change that made all the difference.

I walked into the living room and twirled around like a homecoming princess, smiling so wide my cheeks hurt. This was better than my makeover. I finally felt like me.

Maisy's eyes were wide. "Mom, you changed the color!"

Mrs. Winters smiled and held up her hands. "I texted Heather last night and she told me to do whatever I needed to make it a dress Bea would feel beautiful in. I had a color stripping kit from one of the plays. It was a gamble, but I think it was worth it. Don't you?"

"It's the color of ballet slippers," I said.

I hugged Mrs. Winters. "Thank you."

"Bea, it's perfect. You look stunning," Maisy said.

I met Maisy's eyes. "It's all because of your mom."

Maisy reached out and squeezed my hand twice.

———.———

Mom pulled up to the curb in front of the church. She rolled down her window and we inhaled the smell of the freshly cut grass and wildflowers.

"It's so nice that your father has found someone," Mom said.

I could hear the sadness in her voice.

"I'm the reason he broke up with you," I said, my voice cutting through the church bells.

Mom looked at me. "I know."

"Mr. Pembrook told you?"

"I figured it out," Mom said, with a wry half smile.

"Then why aren't you guys back together?" I asked. "You were so happy with him."

"That's exactly it," Mom said. "Things were so great with Gavin that I didn't really think through things. I think you were right. It was too much too soon."

I nodded. "I get it. I kind of did the same thing with the M & Ms. I was so excited to be part of the popular group that I kind of forgot about everything else."

"I guess we're both the kind of people who go all in," Mom said.

"Maybe the best way for you to figure it all out is to give Mr. Pembrook another chance? But maybe he doesn't practically move in with us yet."

Mom laughed. "Have you always been this smart?"

"Not according to my report card," I said.

The church bells picked up as wedding guests started to walk up the steps.

"I better go," I said, even though I wanted to stay right where I was.

"Want me to walk you up there?" Mom offered, even though I knew that was the absolute last thing she wanted to do.

"I'm okay. I heard Veggie Palace is having a special menu tasting. I know a certain vegan math teacher who would love to go with you," I said.

"I'll think about it," Mom said, with a wink.

I opened the car door and stepped onto the sidewalk. I straightened out my dress hem and adjusted the straps.

"Bea, you look beautiful," Mom said. "The most like yourself that I've seen in a long time."

"Thanks, Mom," I said.

I tried to look confident as I walked up the sidewalk toward the church. There were crowds of people standing around talking to each other, but no one said hi to me. I was at my own dad's wedding, and there were people there who didn't even know me.

I took a deep breath and opened the church door. I walked into the side room off the kitchen, where Dad had told me Monica and the girls would be waiting.

Peyton's eyes widened and she grabbed Vivi's arm as soon as she saw me. "Mom, turn around. Bea's here, and you need to see this."

I was ready to defend my new dress and to finally show my new family who I really was, even if that meant Monica got mad at me or—even worse—if my dad got mad. If I didn't start being myself around my new family, they would never know the real me. I was done being fake to make other people happy.

Monica turned around. Layers of white tulle draped perfectly around her. Her jaw dropped when she saw me. She clasped her hands together.

I braced myself. I could take whatever she said. It was now or never.

"Oh, Bea. You look absolutely breathtaking. I love what you've done with the dress," Monica said.

Peyton and Vivi looked at each other, their eyes wide.

"You're not mad?" I asked.

"You have your own sense of style and you're not afraid to show it," Monica said. "I knew we had something special in common. I just didn't know what it was until now."

In that moment, I realized it was time for me to let Monica and my dad get to know the real me.

MAISY

I watched as Mom scooped up the scraps of fabric and tiny pins off the floor. Mom had always been a sewing magician, but nothing else had been as important as Bea's dress—not even my Dorothy costume from *The Wizard of Oz*.

Mom looked up. "Hey, Maisy. Since you're already standing there, can you help me get this stuff off the floor?"

I walked into the room and got down on my hands and knees and worked on getting some of the tiny needles out of the floorboard cracks.

"You know I usually work much neater than this," Mom said, while she dropped a stack of pale pink fabric in her scrap bag. "But I've never been on a deadline quite like this one before."

I could feel the tips of my ears tinged red with shame. My voice came out throaty and thick. "I was so mean to you at Addy's meet. I humiliated you in front of everyone. I accused you of things you haven't done. Why would you help me and Bea?"

Mom put the garbage bag down. "First of all, Bea's dress was a travesty. There was no way I could let that poor girl walk down the aisle looking like that."

I couldn't help laughing. "It was pretty bad, wasn't it?"

"She looked like she was on her way to a Sweet Sixteen circa 1985 wearing a dress from the bargain bin," Mom said.

I looked down at scattered pins on the floor. "So you didn't help Bea for me then?"

"I did it for you, too." Mom took a long sip of coffee. "To show you the real me is still here."

"Why was I the last person to figure that out?" I asked.

Mom caught my eye. "I never expected you to come around as fast as everyone else in the family. I knew you would need your time and space to figure things out."

"Why did you know it would be different for me?" I asked.

"One thing I learned from therapy is that I am a sensitive soul. I feel things on a deeper level than most people. And sometimes that's a good thing. Like I could feel Bea's pain the second she came in the house. I reminded myself of that when I was tempted to give up halfway through the dress when the stitches were coming apart and I stabbed my fingers with the sewing machine needle for the hundredth time." She wiggled her two pointer fingers, which were wrapped up with Band-Aids.

"But other times, feeling things is just so damn hard." She paused. "And Maisy, I know that you feel things that way, too."

I nodded and breathed out all of the air that had been trapped in my chest. "I really do."

"Your dad takes after Grandma, and Addy takes after both of them. They feel things, but not in the same way we do. They don't get anxious. They don't overthink things. They don't run through scenarios in their minds over and over again," Mom said.

I groaned. "I am so jealous of them."

Mom nodded. "Me too. They just decide they're going to feel a certain way and then they do. They all decided to forgive me and move on, and so they did. I know it wasn't quite that simple, but I never expected you to move on the way they did."

"So you're saying that you forgive me for not forgiving you?" I asked, feeling hot tears creep into the corners of my eyes.

Mom pulled me in to her. She wrapped her arms around me, and I felt something open up deep inside me. The harder I cried, the tighter Mom held on to me.

⪼⋯ CHAPTER TWENTY-NINE ⋯⪻

Three Weeks Later
BEA

AS I WALKED INTO THE KITCHEN, I INHALED THE UNMISTAKABLE
aroma of buttermilk pancakes fresh off the griddle. Mr. Pebbles ran
into the kitchen ahead of me and swatted at Mom's feet.

"This cat is so spoiled," Mom said. She leaned down and gave him
a piece of pancake.

"Pancakes on a school day?" I sat down at the table and drizzled
real maple syrup on my stack. "What's the occasion?"

Mom spun her laptop around. It was open to the bright blue school
portal screen. "Three weeks into second quarter and straight A's!"

"Whoo-hoo!" I shouted.

Last year I wouldn't have thought twice about getting straight
A's because I didn't really need to work for my grades back then. This

time, though, it took hours of extra help before and after school and a lot of studying at home to catch up. Each hour I spent on my schoolwork made me feel closer to who I used to be, closer to who I really am.

Mom poured me a glass of orange juice. "I made enough for Maisy."

I swallowed the big bite of fluffy pancake I had just shoveled in my mouth. "She's eating breakfast at home. We're meeting at school."

"Is everything okay with you girls?" Mom asked. "Maisy hasn't been coming over as often."

"It's all good. She's just spending more time with her family," I said.

Mom made a big show of holding up her Luke's Diner mug so the logo was right in front of my face. "Speaking of family time. Do you know what tonight is?"

"Let me guess . . . we're finally having our *Gilmore Girls* marathon," I said.

Mom nodded. "It's about time!"

"What about Mr. Pembrook? He hasn't been over for a few days," I asked.

"One more day won't make a difference," Mom said. "But I made him that vegan banana bread he's obsessed with. Do you mind dropping it off at his classroom?"

Mr. Pebbles jumped in my lap and I gave him another piece of pancake. "Sure. Last time I went to his classroom, he taught me this really cheesy math rap that I couldn't get out of my head. But it actually helped me on my last test."

Mom laughed. "He taught me a really cheesy rap about how to use the Apple TV. Of course, it worked."

"No wonder you stopped asking me to show you how to do it," I said.

We both laughed, and it felt really good. Like we were getting back to normal.

My phone pinged.

From: Monica
To: Bea

You up for dinner and a movie 🎦 night this weekend? First weekend your dad is off and girls don't have tournaments 😌 Harry Potter 👊 and sushi 🍣 sound good?

Being myself was going to require baby steps.

From: Bea
To: Monica

Harry Potter sounds great! 😃 🖤 TBH I hate sushi. 🍣 🤢

From: Monica
To: Bea

🍥 How's pizza? 🍕

Perfect 👍 Can't wait 🖤

MAISY

"It's been three weeks," I hissed at Mom as soon as I got down to the kitchen. "When is Addy going to stop being mad at me? I've apologized a hundred times. I haven't complained when she's loud in the morning, even though she wakes me up way too early. I haven't even said anything about her leaving her dirty clothes on the floor next to the hamper instead of putting them in the hamper."

Mom smiled at me and handed me a plate with one of her infamous breakfast sandwiches. "You'll know when she's ready."

"It feels like it's taking forever," I said. I pulled out my chair and sat at the table.

Dad smirked over his coffee cup. "Now you know how your mom felt."

"Very funny," I said.

Addy bounced into the kitchen, grabbed a breakfast sandwich off the counter, and took a huge bite before she sat down. I held back on commenting about her nonexistent table manners.

Grandma walked in behind Addy and poured herself a cup

of coffee. She brought her coffee to the table and sat down. "I have news," she announced.

My stomach felt all fluttery. "Grandma, the last time you had news, you stole my room."

"On that topic, I think you all could use a little space and so could I. So I'm moving out," Grandma said, folding her hands in front of her like she always does when she means business.

Dad furrowed his brow. "But you love it here in Mapleton, Mom. You joined the senior center, you're in that book club. You've been talking about taking a watercolor class at the adult school."

"And you love coming to practice," Addy jumped in. "All the girls love your Facebook Stories from the gym."

"I didn't say I was leaving Mapleton. Heather found me an apartment in that beautiful complex over on Maple Heights. So I can still spend plenty of time around here." She looked at Mom. "And I'm always close by anytime you need me."

"We're going to miss having you here twenty-four-seven, Mom, but that complex is beautiful," Dad said.

Mom walked over to Grandma. She wrapped her in a hug and whispered something. Grandma whispered back. They stayed in the hug for what seemed like forever. Then Mom stood up with a teary smile.

"Does that mean Maisy has her room back?" Addy asked.

Grandma smiled. "Yes."

Addy ran over and hugged me.

I hugged her back. "Does this mean you don't hate me anymore?"

Addy laughed. "You are going to be *so* much easier to get along with when you're not reorganizing my leotard drawer."

I laughed.

"But just don't get any ideas about coming to my meet next week," Addy said.

———•———

A few hours later, Bea asked, "Are you ready?"

"I think so," I said, while we walked down the noisy hall. "Are you sure we shouldn't eat in the library again with Clark and the guys?"

"Speaking of Clark . . ." Bea said, in a sing-songy voice.

"I told you it's only as friends."

Bea smirked. "Going to the movies on a Friday night just the two of you sounds like more than friends to me."

I felt a smile creep on my face. "Okay, maybe it's more than friends. We'll see."

Bea grabbed my arm. "You better text me as soon as you get home. I want all the details."

"You know you could always double date with us. I'm sure Griffin or Marshall . . ."

Bea smacked my arm playfully. "Very funny."

I stopped walking. "Are you sure we should go to the cafeteria? I don't know about this."

"I spent a year hiding out in the library. Then I spent a whole quarter hiding behind the M & Ms. I'm done hiding." Bea stopped in front of the cafeteria door. "And so are you."

I took a deep breath and walked toward the small empty picnic table in the back. I sat down first. Bea sat down across from me and unwrapped her tuna sandwich.

"Guess it's a good thing we're sitting by ourselves," I said.

Bea held up a pickle. "Want one?"

I laughed and took the pickle.

At first I wondered if the M & Ms were staring at us from high up on their perch. Then, I realized it wasn't important. I had never felt lonelier than when I sat surrounded by all those fake friends. With Bea, I felt safe and seen, and I was pretty sure she felt the same way.

THE END

ACKNOWLEDGMENTS

AN AUTHOR'S NAME ON A BOOK COVER DOESN'T TELL THE WHOLE story. Luckily, this space allows me to thank all of the people who supported me behind the scenes.

Thank you to Lauren Galit and Caitlen Rubino-Bradway of the LKG Agency for helping me realize that my standalone book was actually a series. This second book wouldn't be here without your vision. Lauren, thank you for always helping me look ahead to the next book and for believing in my future in this industry.

Special thanks to Running Press Kids editor Allison Cohen for being in my corner every step of the way. Your perceptive feedback, endless encouragement, and appreciation for Maisy and Bea meant everything to me. I am incredibly grateful to Senior Project Editor Amber Morris, who made everything about this process as stress-free as possible and kept this anxious writer calm. I always feel like my books and I are in good hands with you at the helm. I am also grateful to Julie Matysik, who stepped in so seamlessly to help get this book out in the world. I am very lucky to have been paired up with Christina Palaia again for copy edits because I know if there is a mistake, she will catch it. Thank you to Lisa K. Weber for once again capturing the personalities of Maisy and Bea in the cover art and chapter illustrations. You brought my imagination to the page with your stunning artwork. Thank you to the rest of the team for all of your hard work—Janelle DeLuise, Valerie Howlett, Hannah Jones, Hannah Koerner, Isabella Nugent, and Marissa Raybuck.

I am immensely grateful to Kathleen Carter of Kathleen Carter Communications for always being open to new ideas, for keeping your finger on the pulse of the middle-grade book world, and for being supportive every step of the way.

The fact that I was able to finish writing this book while recovering from stomach and esophageal surgery is thanks to my dear friend and writing partner Lea Geller. You got me through several months on a liquid diet and made me believe that not only would I be able to swallow food again but also I would be able to finish this book. Our meetings, endless texts, emails, and phone calls saved me.

This series is about the importance of true and authentic friendship. Thank you to my true friends who have seen me at my most vulnerable and loved me through it. I am so grateful for all of you: Elba Burrowes, Michelle Dawson, Lia Gravier, Julie Latham, Stephanie Lia, Crystal Parham, Mandy Stupart, and Vicki Tatarian.

The writing community is filled with some amazing people who are generous with their time, advice, and support. Thank you to Nancee Adams, Cindy Beer-Fouhy, Pari Berk, Marcia Bradley, Kathy Curto, Camille Di Maio, Patricia Dunn, Jimin Han, Veera Hiranandani, Kwana M. Jackson, Barbara Solomon Josselsohn, Susan Kleinman, Falguni Kothari, Lisa Leshaw, Steven Lewis, Edward McCann, Annabel Monaghan, Sweet Orefice, Cari Pattison,

Melissa Roske, and Susie Orman Schnall, Shawna Lubner and Erin Baker of Emma Westchester, and Samantha Woodruff.

Thank you to the industry professionals who helped raise awareness for The Popularity Pact series: Cindy Adams; Hank Garner of the *Author Stories* podcast; Elizabeth Olesh and Kerri Hayman of the Baldwin Public Library; the staff at Barnes & Noble—Eastchester; the staff at Bronx River Books; Lindsey Hein of *The Illuminate* podcast; Robin Kall of *Reading with Robin* podcast; Ashley Hasty of Hasty Book List; Christina Powers aka @a_politicallyreadgirl; Laurie Friedman, from the Mixed-Up Files of Middle-Grade Authors; Paula Fung of Rye Writes & Bites; Jenna Gavigan, MG Book Village; Suzanne Leopold of Suzy Approved Book Tours; Wendy McLeod MacKnight; MG Book Village; Ann-Marie Nieves; Greg Pattridge of Always in the Middle; Ines Rodrigues and Preeti Singh of the Scarsdale Salon; Melissa Roske of Ask the Author; Susan of Red Canoe Reader; Dorothy Schwab of the Grateful Reader; *Westchester Magazine;* Kim Tomsic; Beth Vrabel; Bonnie Lynn Wagner of *A Backwards Story;* and Maddie White.

The Writing Institute at Sarah Lawrence College is where I found my writing and teaching community. Thank you to Patricia Dunn for giving me the opportunity to combine my two passions in the perfect job. I am grateful for all of my students who inspire me with their drive and dedication. I leave every class energized about writing because of all of you. The biggest gift the Writing Institute has given me is my writing group: Ahmed Asif, Marlena Baraf, Jacqueline

Goldstein, Nancy Flanagan, Rebecca Marks, Nan Mutnick, Jessica Rao, and Ines Rodrigues.

Thank you to my parents, Liz and John, who always encouraged me to think for myself and to follow my own path. This book wouldn't exist without your love and support. Thank you to my mother-in-law, Betsy, for always championing me. I am so grateful to my two sisters Katie and Mary Beth for always being there for me, even if I did get the real Cabbage Patch Doll that one Christmas. Love you both. Thank you to the siblings I have been lucky enough to get over the years through marriage. Your support means everything to me. To my nieces, nephews, and godsons, I know that the world is going to be a better place because of all of you. I love you all very much.

Thank you to my daughter, Molly, who will be away at college by the time this book comes out. Usually it's the mother who helps her kid reach their life goals, but in our case, you have been there for me every step of the way, while conquering your own dreams. Thank you to my husband, Douglas, who has been my biggest supporter since the time you protected me and my big poster board from the rain as we walked across campus. I can't imagine a world without you by my side. A special thank you to my little dog, Oscar, who spends his days curled at my feet while I write. I love our little family.